W9-AXQ-770

WITHOUT
BARBARIANS

WITHOUT BARBARIANS

by Jim Magnuson

McGraw-Hill Book Company

New York   St. Louis   San Francisco   Düsseldorf
Mexico   Panama   Toronto

Book designed by Marcy J. Katz.

Copyright © 1974 by Jim Magnuson.
All rights reserved. Printed in the
United States of America. No part of this publication may be reproduced,
stored in a retrieval system, or transmitted,
in any form or by any means, electronic,
mechanical, photocopying, recording, or otherwise,
without the prior permission of the publisher.

123456789BPBP7987654

Library of Congress Cataloging in Publication Data
Magnuson, Jim.
    Without barbarians.

    I. Title.
PZ4.M1876Wi [PS3563.A352]   813'.5'4   74-7457
ISBN 0-07-039506-3

Excerpt from "Waiting for the Barbarians," by C. P. Cavafy from
SIX POETS OF MODERN GREECE, translated by Edmund Keeley
and Philip Sherrard. Copyright © 1960 by Edmund Keeley and Philip
Sherrard. Reprinted by permission of Alfred A. Knopf, Inc.

*I would like to thank Joyce Johnson
and Wendy Weil, whose patience,
encouragement and constant support
have been a central part of the
writing of this book.*

What does this sudden uneasiness mean,
and this confusion? (How grave the faces have become!)
Why are the streets and squares rapidly emptying,
and why is everyone going back home so lost in thought?

> Because it is night and the barbarians have not come.
> And some men have arrived from the frontiers
> and they say that there are no barbarians any longer.

And now, what will become of us without barbarians?
Those people were a kind of solution.

—from "Waiting for the Barbarians"
by C. P. Cavafy, translated by
Edmund Keeley

One

Journal Entry—June 20

*I keep turning it all over in my head—the ambiguities of
involvement and the possibilities of it changing my
whole life in ways I don't consciously want changed—yet
I still cannot make the decision to reject the new. Perhaps
I have made decisions by postponing involvement every
time it comes up. But what is driving me? I can't even
pretend that it is based on some strong personal relationship. What does that make it then, curiosity? It could
only be destructive to my marriage, which I think is fantastic, and cruel to the person I love most. I do not know
the answers. Life has never been so confusing to me.*

*I am not good at expressing my real thoughts in writing.
I'm a perfectly articulate reporter, but now that there is
so much turmoil going on inside me I can scarcely write
at all. I am tired, bored, sick of my patterned, well-adjusted
life. Perhaps it's accentuated by the fact that so many
people Gene and I know are about to start off on new
adventures; new jobs, families, new places. Everyone
but us.*

*That is not to say that things are bad. We are doing
things the way we planned them at least now that the
scare about being pregnant is over. We've been in New
York for three years, I'm done with graduate school and
working finally, if being a Poverty bureaucrat in East
Harlem qualifies as work. Gene is finally out of that horri-*

ble job at the Children's Shelter, finding some time to write and his play will be produced this summer. We talk out our problems as honestly as anyone has the right to expect. We are living the kind of life we set out to live.

Then why?

My exposure to people like Daniel and Peter. People who react to the world so differently than I do. It's made me want to experiment, to try strange, new things. Although I'm intellectually a radical I have never lived out anything like a radical existence. Now there is that possibility.

Daniel came into my office yesterday and, after some hemming and hawing, blurted out that he wanted to make love to me. It would have been absolutely appropriate to laugh—it was all so artless and without calculation—but I didn't. Because it would have hurt him, I suppose. There are times that his vulnerability is a marvelous protection. But I can't kid myself—the issue is not settled.

If I only knew why I am so drawn to him. He is five years younger than I am and when I try to tell him some things about my life I feel as if I'm burdening with winter clothes someone who has only known summer. I don't feel the same sexual electricity that I've felt with Peter and at times wonder if it isn't our both being attracted to Peter that has brought Daniel and me together in this way. Daniel is so uncertain of his own sexuality and I wonder about what sort of surrogate figure I'm becoming . . . I don't believe that I can be drawn into this so quickly. The more I analyze it, the more complex it becomes. There are moments when I'm not even sure that I like him—he is very selfish and oblivious to the effects that he has on people.

Yet he elates me, excites me the way no one else does. He's probably very bright, but in an odd, quirky way—it awakens things in me, makes me want to experience more, know more—books, music, feelings, whatever—and explore new limits for myself.

Brave words—but then there are the small hypocrisies. I came home and told Gene that I had been propositioned. Perhaps I did it to test how serious it all was, I don't know, but Gene kept pushing me about who it was and finally I lied and said it was Peter. I'm still furious with myself. Why was I so self-protective? It's funny how the small things end up making me guiltier than the big ones. But I'm disappointed in myself for lying, precisely when I want to be most honest and open.

The afternoon that I saw her for the last time I remembered an earlier afternoon when I had come home and found her lying across the bed, crying. Looking back, trying to find the point where things began to go wrong, the first thing that occurs to me is nothing direct or logical, but rather the image of her small, olive hands curved and tensed on the white pillow.

I had stood in the doorway, watching her; a slender body diagonal across the bed, long, dark hair spread loosely, hiding her face from me. It was late afternoon; through the window I could see gray March clouds scudding in a dark sky. What she had just told me hadn't sunk in; all that I heard was her crying.

"Ann . . . Ann, tell me what he said."

She looked up at me. "What could he say? It doesn't matter."

"It does matter. Tell me," I said.

"He said there was no child. It was a mistake. I'm not pregnant, I wasn't pregnant . . . ."

"But the tests . . . ."

"It's as if I made the whole thing up, as if it was nothing but fantasy."

I sat down on the bed and, reaching out, brushed the hair away from her face. She pulled away, leaning up against the wall, her knees tight to her chest. "Please, don't tell me it's going to be all right," she said. "I don't want to hear it."

We sat without speaking, looking directly at one another. My gaze broke and I looked away from her. I felt like an intruder. A few weeks ago, when she first thought she was pregnant, I had felt somehow superfluous to the event; now, knowing that I wasn't to be a father, I felt doubly so.

The violence of her reaction frightened me; it didn't make sense. We hadn't planned to have the child, it had been a mistake. We had come to New York with a well-thought-out plan: I found a job with the Welfare Department to support us while Ann went to graduate school; when she finished she would work and I would write. At some later point, after we had accomplished some of the things we had set out to do, we would have a child.

It was a good, solid plan and it had been working. Ann was bright, ambitious and a brilliant student. We had little money and most of the time we felt out of breath, but we were proud of one another, we talked through problems as they came up, and the affection we felt seemed clear and deep.

An unexpected pregnancy should have been a disaster.

All our plans were shot; we would have to borrow money, I would have to stay at a job I was starting to hate, we were up against it. Yet Ann was excited by it, perhaps precisely because it was disruptive and unplanned.

We had been keeping it a secret; it was too soon to be sure. Sharing the same fears and expectancies, telling no one, we grew closer than we had ever been in our marriage. We craved the time we had with one another, knowing how radically things would have to change. Then, a week ago, she had started spotting and having cramps. She had made an appointment to see the doctor.

She lowered her knees and sat unmoving, head bowed, an isolated figure against the white wall. "I was so sure there was something there. Something in me . . . and now he says that it never was."

"Ann, it's no one's fault," I said.

"I just feel so cheated!" she said.

"But if we could have had things just the way we wanted them, Ann, would it be any different? We're where we were before."

"No, we're not. We're not."

She threw herself back down on the bed, resting her face on the back of my hand. With my other hand I stroked her shoulder. We had so narrowly escaped the beginning of something that neither of us thought we wanted; now we were grieving that loss as if it were the only thing in our lives. The child had been no more than an idea, a phantom, yet it had found its depth in her like an anchor tossed to the bottom of a lake.

"Nothing's happened, Ann. Hey, look here. Tomorrow's Sunday. We'll go over to your parents' for dinner."

"I thought it was your Sunday to go to work," she said.

I remembered and grimaced. "Oh, Jesus."

8

She smiled. "It's not that bad, is it?"

"Just on Sundays," I said. "No, I'm tough. Real tough."

She laughed at me. "Sure, you are."

"Okay," I said. "You go over to your parents for dinner. Forget about studying for once. Give yourself a day off." I got up from the bed. I picked up the bottle of vitamins from the bedside table and set it down again. "We're all right. Nothing's happened. Honest. Honest."

He sat crouched on the visiting bench, glaring at me like a small fierce bird, his eyes glittering oddly in his lean, eroded face. His name was Gonzalez, I had it down in the book. Patches of matted black hair erupted in all directions from his head. He wore a faded Hawaiian shirt and his shoes were a tattered two-tone plastic. He was jammed between other waiting parents, next to a black mother who hovered protectively over her child at the end of the bench. Children dashed by on their way to the water fountain, their shouts echoing down the long yellow hallway. In the midst of all the confusion Gonzalez did not blink an eye or utter a word.

Someone stepped across my line of vision. I looked up from my desk. The tall pale man in front of me seemed to recoil as if he had made some mistake. One long hand trembled in front of his face. When he saw that I had noticed he pulled the hand quickly away.

"Your name?" I asked.

"Barnes. Robert Barnes."

"Address?"

"Two Eleven . . . Two Eleven East Thirty-second."

"Your relationship to the child?" A high-pitched shriek reverberated down the hall as he spoke. I saw his lips move but wasn't able to hear him. "I'm sorry," I said. "I didn't hear . . ."

He blinked, grimaced. "I'm his father."

I entered it all neatly in the big frayed visitor's book. "Fine. If you'll just take a seat I'll send someone up to get him."

"I can't go up to see him?"

"He'll be down. It will just take a couple of minutes. I'm sorry, I don't make the rules." Stupid words coming out of my mouth, but the only ones at my disposal.

"I heard he was sick. Do you know if he was sick?"

"No, I don't."

"I just wanted . . . ." He stared at me for a second, then his eyes faltered and he headed, slump-shouldered, off to the bench, a bag of candy swinging loosely at his side.

Gonzalez intently watched the children visiting their parents in the lobby. A child of two toddled up to him, put his hands on his knee and burbled something. There was a flicker of response in Gonzalez's face, then he caught my eye, and glared back.

"Your name, please."

"Maan of God." A thick Jamaican accent.

"What?"

"Maan of God."

I took a deep breath. I hadn't had a single straight answer all afternoon. My pen rested on the visitor's book. Was I really expected to write this down?

Miss Hernandez, sitting beside me, leaned over. "It's Reverend Wren. Kevin and David, B-5. Just put it down and don't bother with the questions. He's mad. Don't mess around."

I looked up at Reverend Wren. "Address?" I asked, smiling.

"I'm not a man of this world." I did a double take. He had delivered that line completely deadpan. A black Buster Keaton posing as the Messiah. I couldn't resist.

"Not of this world?"

"No."

"Well, whatever world it is . . . ." I saw Miss Hernandez flash me a warning glance. "We'd like an address."

There was no response. He was staring off over my head. I looked around. There was no one there.

Miss Hernandez muttered, "I told you."

"Reverend Wren?"

"Yes?"

"I'll send for your boys."

The entire week built to Sunday, visiting day. Sunday was the test. Either they came or they didn't. There was no chance for faking it, no more fantasies about the rich grandfather, the kindly aunt, the father returning from Puerto Rico. The boys would all dress up in the cheap suits the Welfare Department had allotted them, smooth out their wrinkled ties, and wait. They would play cards in their dorm, lie on their beds watching the football game on TV, waiting for the runner to come up with a pass that meant they had a visitor. Only a few, those that had been in the shelter for a year, year and a half, and longer, were hardened enough to pretend they didn't care.

Mr. Gonzalez leapt off the bench suddenly as a trio of boys came tripping noisily down the stairs. As if he thought one of them was his son. It wasn't. He paced up and down, lit a cigarette. Glaring at me. I tried to remember what dorm his son was in, but the woman in front of me was waiting. I wrote out a pass and handed it to the eleven-year-old runner, who dashed quickly up the stairs. I turned to the next person in line.

There was not enough room. Not room enough to walk, to play, to say the things that needed to be said. The tiled lobby, echoing with noise, was jammed. A brother and sister talked shyly in a corner, eyes darting to the guards that were prominently stationed at the doors. An old woman, eyes closed, rocked a seven-year-old grandson in her long skirts, moving a lock of hair from his eyes as he talked. A thin, battered woman tried to put a toy together for her son, her hands shaking, until someone brushed by and the pieces clattered to the floor. She cursed and ran to the bathroom. A father, intimidated by the noise and the crowd, held his son's hand and stared at the children's drawings taped to the wall, saying nothing.

Their stories were no secret. The kids would tell us, and case records were never as confidential as the Welfare Department wanted people to believe. Everyone got the stories down: Mrs. Gardner who stuck her son in the oven, nearly burning him to death. After a spell at Manhattan State she was released and showed up at the Center every Sunday, faithfully. She fluttered over him, trying to please him, to make him forgive, her white moon face almost comically vulnerable. The burns scarcely showed on the boy any more, arcs and splotches of red that might have been caused by a long afternoon at the beach. Still he would flinch when her hand flitted up to her streaked gray white hair. Freddy Jefferson's father, debonair and immaculately dressed, carrying himself through the crowds like an English lord bereft of his carriage. He told me once that he was a head chef in a big hotel downtown, it was merely a misunderstanding that landed Freddy in the Center, yet Freddy had been in the Center for five months and was one of the baddest-assed kids there. He would sit listening sullenly to his father's elegant talk and then walk back up the stairs without a word or a backward glance. There was Mr. O'Neill, one-legged ex–racecar driver and bigamist, choler-faced, energetically swinging his way up the stairs on crutches to shout at us. There were child-beaters, petty thieves, prostitutes and small-time gangsters, but sitting in the lobby talking awkwardly with a child they seemed much less sensational than their case histories.

Mr. Gonzalez stood up, put out his cigarette, gestured to me. I didn't understand what he wanted. Frowning, he moved forward, pushing his way through the line of waiting people.

"Mr. Gonzalez, these people . . . ."

"Where's my kid? Huh?"

"Mr. Gonzalez . . . ."

"Where is he?"

"I sent up the pass. I don't know."

"I've been waiting for forty-five minutes."

"I'm sorry. I don't know."

"Forty-five minutes."

"I'll send someone up to check, all right?"

"Where is he, huh?" It irritated me that he had to repeat everything two and three times. Behind him were others in line, moving uneasily, straining to see what was happening.

"Look, what do you want me to do? Did you hear what I said? I'll send someone upstairs to find out what happened." He gave no response. He wasn't even looking at me. "Okay? Please sit down."

Five minutes later one of the runners came down and handed me a note. Hector Gonzalez wasn't in the dorm. He had gone out on Saturday on a weekend pass with his mother. I cursed, feeling my face flare red. The runner looked at me curiously.

"Then how come it's not in the book?" I demanded.

The runner shrugged.

I slumped back, clutching the arms of my chair. Miss Hernandez frowned.

"Oh God . . . what do I do?"

"You better tell him," she said. "Waiting isn't going to help."

"Ya?"

"Ya," she said, imitating my midwestern twang.

I got up from behind the desk and walked slowly across the room, dodging a small boy who darted from the water cooler, his cheeks bulging with water. Gonzalez looked up, waiting for me.

"Mr. Gonzalez . . . Mr. Gonzalez, I'm very sorry. There's been a mix-up. The boy just told me that Hector went out yesterday. On a weekend pass with his mother. I'm very sorry. They didn't make any note of it. We had no way of knowing."

"He what?"

"He's not here. He went out on a pass."

Gonzalez looked at me with contempt. "You're lying to me, man. Why did you keep me waiting?"

"I didn't know. There wasn't any record of it. Someone forgot to make an entry . . . ."

"You make me sit for an hour, man, then you tell me . . . ."

"I'm very sorry. I know it's . . . ." I felt myself wriggling like a speared fish.

"Who said he could go out? Huh? You say so, man?"

"No. There's a social worker who decides that. I have nothing to do . . . ."

"Who is it?"

"Who is what?"

"The social worker. The social worker."

"I don't know. You should know that."

"But I don't know, man. I'm just a stupid Puerto Rican. And you're here. Right? Right?" He waited for an answer.

"Ya, I'm here," I said.

"Well, you know what you did? You let the kid go out with a whore. A drug addict, man. You so smart." People had gathered around us, forming a gawking wall. I turned to go but he grabbed my arm. "Don't you walk away when I'm talking to you. I want to talk to somebody."

"Just take your hand off me . . . man," I said. I stared at him. "Take it off." He obeyed. "Now if you want to talk to somebody you can go down to Two Fifty Church Street tomorrow and have it out with the social worker . . . ."

"You gonna give me carfare?" I stared at him, dumbfounded. "I want to talk to somebody now!"

"You go down there and talk to the social worker. I didn't have anything to do with this."

"That's a bunch of bullshit."

I turned away, not even bothering to reply. I heard him say something in Spanish that I didn't understand, but the tone was clear enough. I kept walking, smiled, let go a quick, frustrated snort. Suddenly Gonzalez was up beside me, his eyes wild and angry.

"Are you laughing at me?"

"No. I'm not laughing at you."

"You were laughing at me."

"No."

"I saw you, man!"

A large black woman stood up and pointed at me, threatening as an Uncle Sam recruiting poster. "I saw him too. I saw him laugh."

Gonzalez's voice seemed to constrict with emotion. "You making fun of me? What is it that's so funny? No comprendo."

"There's nothing funny at all."

A crowd was closing in around us, pushing forward, tightening, accusations thrown back and forth. Reverend

Wren raised a magisterial black hand over us but his words were lost in the babble. A security guard tried to move through the mob.

"No, there's nothing funny about it, man. Wait till it happens to you, wait till they steal your kids, social worker, wait till you get fucked over . . . ."

"Hey, buddy . . . ." The voice of the guard seemed to trigger Gonzalez. I saw Gonzalez move and I half-turned, catching the hurried blow on my shoulder. Instinctively my arm went up. I saw Gonzalez start, but I had him, I was going to smash him . . . . He knew it, I could see it in his face. Then I froze. Suddenly I was confused. We stared at one another, not even for a second, before the guard had him and it was all over. Someone came over to break up the crowd. I brought my hand up to feel my shoulder and realized that I was shaking.

They let me off early. Outside the Center the street was jammed with cars, double- and triple-parked. Counselors and kids leaned against the rough brick building, bathed in spring sunlight. A group was coming in from the park, all in sweatshirts and dirty jeans, one or two boys in over-sized football helmets that wobbled when they ran. A boy darted out between the cars for a pass, the football spiraled just beyond his reach and skipped with a bang off the roof of a car. I put my head down and walked.

I moved briskly across the park at 110th Street as the sun faded in the trees. All the Number Four buses were full, grinding and lurching their way crosstown. On the park side of the street there were only quiet old men, heads down, some with bottles, some not. I started to jog.

I hadn't lied to him. I hadn't known. How could he blame me for losing his kid? He was crazy; if you started hitting people every time you lost something . . . . Shit. I felt as if I'd hit an oil slick going full-speed.

It was a long way back. I walked up past the jumble of garages and auto shops, past people sitting on the stoops, past Morningside Park. Everything seemed far away, odd, the way you might feel when looking for the first time at a film of a foreign country. The setting sun seemed to dissolve in a polluted wash of color, but the hard, etched features of Gonzalez remained. Suddenly I had to see Ann, I had to know that she was all right. I began to run. When I reached Broadway, I was out of breath and slowed again to a walk.

I turned in at 116th Street, the wind off the river rushing up the graceful curve of buildings. Entering Claremont there was a sudden hush, as if a door had firmly and discretely been closed on the noise of the city. A pipe-smoking, middle-aged man polished his car with infinite care. Twin blond girls wobbled by on their bicycles, under the watchful eyes of the uniformed black doormen.

I rang the doorbell and waited. One . . . two . . . three . . . then footsteps. Ann opened the door. She looked surprised.

"You're back early."

"Yup."

I held her, kissed her, hiding my face from her. She pulled away and looked at me, her quick blue eyes searching for something, not quite finding it.

"Is something wrong?" she asked.

"No. Are you all right?"

"Yes. I'm fine." She put her hands up to mine, took both of them away. The bones in her hands were small and fragile. When she spoke again her voice was firm. "Do you want something to eat?"

"Sure."

Together we walked down the long, softly carpeted hallway, light still pouring through the French windows.

In the living room Mr. Spiros was stretched out in his black leather chair watching TV golf, his eyes half-open under dark, bushy eyebrows, the picture of the Greek patriarch. Ann's mother, sitting at an ironing board at the other end of the spacious room, looked up, smiled, went back to her ironing.

I sat down on the couch while Ann went into the kitchen. Cary Middlecoff filled the TV screen, whispering about some enormous sum of money, and then the camera cut away, trying to follow the white golf ball as it sailed into the white TV sky. I lost it. I got up, went to the windows, and opened them. Far below were the Barnard tennis courts, white-skirted girls batting the ball easily back and forth. I could hear the pong of the ball hitting the racket even as the shadows from the high buildings crept silently across the green courts.

Ann brought out a bowl of her father's soup and set it on the dining-room table. I ate alone, sipping a glass of red wine. Ann sat in the living room reading a book, her father had fallen asleep in his chair. Her mother was ironing by the windows where you could look out and see the sun glint off the Hudson. A scene of domestic tranquility that wasn't to be for very much longer; her parents were going to London for a year where he was to teach in a medical school. But still I wasn't able to value it, honor it, not right then. There was a cold, angry knot in my stomach.

Ann looked up, sensing something wrong. She put down her book and came to the table.

"Now?" she asked.

"Now what?"

"Are you going to tell me now?"

"No. When we go."

"When do you want to go?"

"Now."

"All right."

Ann got up, made excuses to her mother, who looked a bit startled. I waited, not bothering to invent anything, just said good-by. When Ann had kissed her father good-by I scooped up her books and we left.

It seemed cold as winter walking down Broadway in the early evening. Steam rose in eerie clouds from the sewers in the street. A Columbia cop huddled in the doorway of the West End Bar. We walked briskly to get out of the cold, yellow cabs careening by, empty.

The first thing I did when we got home was take a shower. Afterward, standing in the hallway, rubbing my head with a towel, I watched her writing in her journal. She sat at her desk, very erect, with a look of almost child-like solemnity, completely absorbed. I watched her hand move decisively across the page. I kept my distance, not wanting to interrupt; I feel an almost pristine stillness in catching her unaware of me. Finally she looked up.

"Tell me what's wrong," she said.

"It wasn't so great a day," I said.

"Then tell me," she said. I told her. About Gonzalez, how he had sat there waiting, about how he had pushed his way through the line, how he had hit me.

"I nearly swung at him," I said.

"There's nothing very unnatural in that," she said.

"No? It made me sick afterward. What am I going to hit him for? For being a loser? He's never gonna get his kid back. The guy keeps getting arrested for creating disturbances in Welfare Centers. So I'm going to punch the guy out."

"Hey, come on. I thought this kind of stuff didn't get to you."

"What the hell am I doing in this city?"

"Would you come here?" she said. She took my hands and put them around her waist. "I love you," she said. "I love you."

"I know that," I said.

"I'm sorry about yesterday. It was stupid. It was completely irrational."

"Maybe it wasn't."

"We weren't ready, Gene. Not to be parents."

"I know."

"Please. I hate it when you're depressed. Things will be getting better for us. Once I get out of school, I'll be working. I talked to the people at my field placement office and they want me to stay on full-time at the settlement house after I graduate. You'll be able to quit that place, you'll have time to write."

"That's not the point, Ann."

"But it is. There's no reason why we should lead ordinary lives. We can make our own rules, Gene."

I listened to her talk, unbelieving. She couldn't have shaken it all so quickly, yet it seemed that something had closed up in her. Maybe she was being brave; I just didn't know.

"Dry your hair," she said. "You'll catch cold."

"I'm sorry. Just one of those bad moods."

"Come on, let's go to bed. I've got to get up for school tomorrow."

I lay on the bed watching her undress. The lights from cars passing below on Broadway flickered shadows against the curtain.

"Did I tell you I met the new VISTAs on Friday?" she said.

"No."

"They're assigning three of them to the settlement house. I'll probably be supervising them. God, they seem so young."

"Where are they from?"

"One guy from Michigan and two from California. A very strange kid from L.A. named Daniel. Very shy. I can't imagine how they'll survive in East Harlem. Let me brush my teeth."

When she left the room I stared at the alternation of light and dark on the window. For a moment I imagined I saw Gonzalez there, perched on the window ledge, waiting patiently for a child that would never come, that had been torn forever from him.

Ann came in and slipped into bed alongside me. I turned to her, wanting to say something.

"Hey," she said, "it's fine. I'm so happy. I'm so happy just to be married to you." My body was still cold from the shower, but I held her, curling her body into mine, till both of our bodies were warm. She fell asleep first, turning away from me. I lay there alone for a minute, then pressed my face deep into her dark hair, smelling its cleanness, feeling its softness, blindly pushing away all phantoms and shadows till I joined her in sleep.

Journal Entry—June 25

I don't know if I can write at all. A week of internal struggle and lots of discussion with Gene about our marriage, its problems and joys, the new dimensions our life may take, the anxiety of the unknown, and yet I knew, even as we talked that I—we—are going to plunge into it. Maybe I'm frightened, but after seeing Daniel on Friday and talking to Gene Friday night I feel elated— a burden lifted, somehow a new life is possible now, I am really going to break out of old patterns, self-imposed rules and regulations and those imposed by society which I do not need. I am going to try not to be totally selfish in this, Gene is part of it too. We talked about conflict arising, we're ready for that, as much as we can be ready. Perhaps we'll hurt one another, but we will share, talk, be honest. We're striving for a certain amount of freedom and that's for both of us, trying to let the other breathe, walk around and look at the world through their own eyes. Marriage means giving up some things, making compromises, but need it mean always trying to possess the other, trying to live through the other person? We're two separate people. I hope we can be open to other relationships without fear, guilt and suspicion. It will not be easy, but we're going ahead. I really feel the fullness of life right now and the joy of expectation of new experience ahead without the bonds and rigidities, all the moral stop and go signs of the past. Free . . . .

She wanted to live without the bonds of the past. It seemed to me that they were being broken without our making the choice. I would have chosen differently if I'd been able to.

My mother's father came from Sweden with his brothers just before the turn of the century. They went to western Minnesota and worked for years clearing land; cutting trees, ripping out the stumps, selling the firewood, creating room for wheat on the rolling hills. They were frugal, hardworking, and when they had saved enough money they bought land of their own, my grandfather leaving his brothers to buy a farm in North Dakota, just west of Fargo.

He brought with him a hired man, a shy young man from my grandfather's home town in Sweden and just off the boat. When he arrived Emil scarcely spoke five words of English. Together they worked the farm hard, did well, began to accumulate cattle, more land, full bins of wheat. My grandfather married a sternly religious young woman, they had four children, three girls and a boy, my mother being the middle girl. With their hard work came a steady, inevitable progress; many years later I was shown pictures of the huge threshing crews, gangs of twenty, thirty men brought in for the harvest. Spurred on by his successes my grandfather opened a brick kiln. Years later, the kilns were still there on the farm, obscured by cottonwoods and thistles and rusting farm machinery. In the older sections of Fargo and Grand Forks you can find the worn imprint of my grandfather's name in the brick sidewalks.

My grandfather was killed while driving a milk wagon into town. A backfiring car frightened the horses and when they bolted he was thrown under the wheels of the wagon. It was the beginning of the Depression and all the children were still in school. Emil helped carry the family through, he and my uncle Arnold, and my aunt Harriet, who was the oldest daughter, banding together to fill the place of the vigorous father with the red Prussian mustache. It was hard, all the supports that had seemed so solid were crumbling. The kilns were closed, most of the cattle were sold. My aunt Harriet was forced into teaching piano, taking the bus out to small North Dakota towns on Thursday afternoons to run eight-year-olds up and down the scales. It was a struggle.

As difficult as it was, it didn't last. The children grew up. World War Two came and the price of wheat rose.

My father appeared, the tall, gangly, big-jawed son of a Swedish preacher. He had spent his childhood moving from one small country town to another in North Dakota and western Minnesota, listening to thunderous sermons, a preacher's kid, and he wanted to go to college and get out. Instead he married my mother, quit school, got a job in Fargo, had me, my sisters and my brother Matt.

After the death of my grandmother, which I do not remember, the youngest daughter went to California, married a man who worked in an airplane factory in the San Fernando valley.

Left on the farm were Arnold, Harriet, and Emil.

Summers I was sent back to the farm for two- or three-week vacations. It was something I looked forward to. The farm was large, the horizon flat, endless; if you wanted to walk out of sight it would take half a day. It was a jumble of pleasures; a dog, a pond, an abandoned potato cellar, plenty of chickens and pigeons to chase, the old kilns, a horse, a granary, and a windmill that rattled in the strong prairie winds that seemed to blow all day long. When I was lucky Emil would lift me up on the horse and prod it around the yard. I'd twine my hands firmly in the mane and thump the horse in the ribs with my heels, shouting as loudly as if I was leading a cavalry charge.

With no children of their own my aunt and uncle showed no shame about spoiling me. When I felt like drawing, Harriet supplied me with large sections of sturdy posterboard and thick pencils. I remember sitting in the cool of the empty icehouse when it was blistering hot outside, sneezing sawdust and drawing enormous murals of cowboy–Indian battles.

I was a fan of the Indians all the way and in my drawings they never lost a battle. In my elaborately constructed pictures one lone Indian would often be flipping Custer over his shoulder with one arm, tomahawking a soldier with the other, and drop-kicking a third. My art was morally unsubtle, but ingeniously devised.

I stubbornly resisted the historical fact that the Indians

had lost. The land had been theirs first. This land. It was Sioux land, even as I heard my uncle's tractor plowing in a far field. I tried to imagine it, looking out as far as I could see, a group of horsemen on the horizon, shimmering like a mirage at first, then growing larger, more distinct, till I could make out their headdresses and buckskin jackets, feathers and beads, their bows and spears, eyes fierce and angry as they wheeled their horses through the fields of grain, trampling wide swaths of wheat.

One afternoon I found an old book buried in the piles of newspapers and back numbers of the *Reader's Digest*, *Farm and Home*, and *The Country Gentleman* that my aunt stored in the pantry. It was a history of the Plains Indians, full of drawings, maps, and fuzzy photographs of chiefs and warriors, ponies and campfires. There was an astounding picture of the Sun Dance of the Sioux, in which the young brave, his shoulders pierced with leather thongs, hangs—suspended for days from a tall pole, staring into the sun, waiting for enlightenment as the leather slowly rips his flesh.

The picture affected me deeply. One afternoon, sitting by the pond, I heard a sudden rustling behind me and I spun quickly, positive that I would see a young Sioux brave hanging among the glistening silver leaves of the Russian olive trees.

I tried to fit the brave into my childish theological system, but it was hard, since the Sioux were torturing themselves for the Sun God, not the Father of Adam and Eve that I knew. Seated by my bed one night, my Aunt Harriet skillfully reconciled the discrepancies by suggesting that there was one God and we simply called him different names. It made sense. I attempted saying my prayers to the Great Spirit for several nights, but found it unsatisfactory.

As much as there was to do, summer days had a way of stretching on and on without end. Sometimes when I was bored I would go out to the gravel road, throw up pebbles and whack at them with a baseball bat, giving it the Duke Snider Cadillac swing, knock the rock soaring over the barbed wire fence, hitting the Ebbetts Field wall at the 380-foot mark. My sisters and I would pick mint and help my aunt make ice cream, crushing the mint into the swirl of slowly hardening liquid, cranking the handle of the wooden ice-cream bucket till our arms were ready to fall off. I would go to the barn and chase barn rats, throw the pitchfork clattering after them, knowing that I would never hit one. If none of this relieved the boredom of long afternoons I would follow the dog out to the fields, wander aimlessly after him as he sniffed his way through the grain, darting ahead suddenly to scare up grouse and pheasant, leaving a wave of shaking grain in his wake.

There was no one to play with, really. Sisters didn't count and Matt was too young. There were two boys who lived on the edge of town who prowled in our woods from time to time, shooting at birds. One day as I shuffled through the thistles, going nowhere in particular, they popped up out of an abandoned kiln and asked me if I wanted to join them. In the kiln? No, they'd find a new game. They were older than I was. I was honored. I said yes.

We snuck our way into the machine shed, taking a minute to adjust our eyes to the darkness of the huge, musty building, birds squeaking in the shadowy rafters. I followed the two boys up the ladder to the loft. There's our game, they said, pointing to the enormous pulley. It was attached to a giant iron hook. I had seen my uncle use it to hoist heavy farm machinery. The hook was large enough for a small boy to sit comfortably inside it. We were going to take turns riding. I wasn't chicken, was I? I shook my head. No.

They went first, one at a time, swinging out into space on creaking ropes, the two of us left behind cranking the pulley wheel. They seemed extremely brave, riding down into the darkness below us, holding onto the rope with one hand, waving and laughing, then back up again without having flinched once.

It was my turn. I set myself in the curved iron swing, held on tight to the ropes, and out I went, my stomach leaping wildly with fright. Down I went, much too fast, I lost my breath, then up again. With delight I realized that I was safe. Down, I let out an echoing whoop, then up again, the pulley gear rat-tat-tatting as I rose. Down again for a third time and suddenly the hook came to a swaying standstill, like a bucket hitting the water at the bottom of a well. I looked up to where the boys were standing, the light streaming through the gaps in the beamed roof above them.

"What are you guys doing?"

They said nothing. A barn swallow flitted silently across the space and nestled somewhere in the darkness. I looked down. Fifteen feet below me was the dirt floor and the heavy dark shapes of threshers and tractors, huge oil drums and the smell of gasoline. I clung to the pulley rope.

"Pull me up!"

They laughed. "Maybe we will, maybe we won't."

"Let me down then."

"Maybe we will, maybe we won't." Again they laughed, the sound echoing in the cavernous building.

"You can't do this!"

"Why not?"

"This is my uncle's farm! Not yours. It doesn't belong to you . . . ."

"So what?"

I was dizzy and nauseated. Suspended on a giant iron hook, as terrified as Jonathan Edwards' poor spider, I was sure I would retch if it didn't end immediately. I stared down once more. It looked like a long way down, but the ambiguity of hanging there, of not ·knowing, was worse, worse even than crashing into oil drums. I let go of my hold on the rope and fell, arms flailing in a plummeting, heavy flight. I hit my head on a tractor and rattled into unconsciousness.

The two terrified boys ran to tell my uncle, who came and carried me back to the house. I spent the next two days in bed, drinking soup and drawing pictures of long-maned horses. A doctor came to examine me and ordered me back on my feet.

I didn't see the two boys until weeks later when I met them on the road. They were both guilt-ridden and terribly solicitous. We played together for the next several days and got along well.

One Friday the sun was blistering hot, the insects screaming in the long grass. I went with my two new friends to the pond, where we pushed off makeshift boats made of bark and twigs, only to bomb them with rocks, sending up geysers of muddy water. We had sunk half a dozen of our boats when I spied a dark shadow lying just beneath the surface of the water. At first I thought it might be a fish, but it didn't move. I shouted to the others and we found a long pole to poke at it, pushing it slowly toward the shore. It was a heavy burlap bag, perhaps it was filled with treasure, maybe Jesse James had hid it years ago . . . . We hurried down into the mud and yanked the heavy wet bag ashore.

It was tied at one end and the older boy sawed at the twine with his penknife, working so excitedly that he cut his thumb. "Damn!" he yelled, waving it in the air, but we shouted at him and he went back to work, finally slitting the bag open with a flourish.

He looked inside and then looked quickly away, his jaw suddenly slack, his face white.

"Come on! Let us see!" We grabbed for the bag. On first glance I didn't recognize them for what they were; they seemed merely grotesquely bloated bubbles of flesh, the short fur wet and matted. One or two had their teeth carelessly bared in their gaping mouths. The rest seemed to be asleep, curled around one another in the rock-weighted bag. They had been in the pond for a long time; the water had swollen them to twice the size of normal kittens. The stench made my eyes smart. I turned away from the bag.

We let the sack down. No one would touch it. The younger boy began to cry. It was absolutely still, the trees surrounding the pond motionless. Water trickled out of the bag onto the brown, dry grass.

That night I told Harriet what had happened. She explained as best she could: sometimes people will have a litter of kittens that they aren't able to feed and take care of and aren't able to find anyone to take them. They feel they have no choice. They weight a sack with rocks, tie the kittens inside, and throw it in a pond. Then they're done with it. These people, my aunt said, think that it's better to do that than to abandon them, to let them be killed by dogs or grow up wild and stray. I stared at her. I had never liked cats, but what she was saying now was inconceivable.

That night I had a dream. I don't know whether I dreamt that I was a cat or if I dreamt from a cat's point of view, but I remember the rough jostling, the unwanted animals' bodies around me, the hanging feeling in the stomach of being thrown free in space, hitting the water, plunging down and down, water pouring through the burlap in a thousand tiny streams, cats clawing at one another, not cute, fluffy kittens any more, but screaming, biting, dying animals, fighting blind for the disappearing air, tearing at each other's bodies in the darkness, gasping, and then, in surprise, choking, swallowing water . . . .

Emil slept in a bunk house fifty yards from the main house. In the old days there had been other men living there; now it was his alone. When we were very small he would sit in the kitchen after supper, smoke his pipe, and talk to my grandmother in Swedish. After she died he spent more and more time by himself. With the sale of the farm animals there was less to do, and after the purchase of new farm machinery my uncle could handle a lot of the field work alone.

That summer Emil would slouch off every morning to collect eggs from the chicken coop, a task he had always scorned as woman's work. Other times he would take his wooden handled scythe and cut the weeds at the edge of the yard, a tall, bent figure in overalls and striped railroad engineer's hat, working patiently at the same steady pace.

In the winter he decided to go back to Sweden. I was a child, I wasn't included in the discussion. It was explained to me that he wanted to go back to see his relatives a last time, but I sensed that there was something more, there was some hidden bitterness, some dispute over money, or perhaps he just didn't want to die a hired man.

Two weeks before he was supposed to leave he moved out, rented a room downtown. We went to visit him there once, walking quickly down Broad Street in the cold, the black water of the river swirling turgidly by, pocked by rain.

We hurried through a high-ceilinged lobby that was nearly deserted. Two men coughing and chewing on pipes sat playing a slow game of cards. A fifty-year-old woman with swollen legs, her face blotched like badly stained leather, sat reading the Sunday comics on an overstuffed couch.

We walked up two flights of stairs and knocked at a half-opened door. Emil opened the door quickly, yet seemed startled to see us. He was wearing a blue suit. I had never seen him in anything but overalls before and he seemed much smaller now. He didn't quite know what to do with us and seemed embarrassed by his small, drab room. We sat on the edge of the bed, my little brother looking at the pictures in the Gideon Bible. Emil gave short, perfunctory answers to questions about his trip, rubbing his long, white face, never looking at anyone directly. When my father suggested that we all go out for coffee, Emil accepted.

On the street Emil walked to one side, holding my little brother's hand, but saying nothing, staring absently at store windows. He was not at all rude, but he was already separating himself from us.

The rest is a story told to me by adults. He boarded a train in Fargo that was taking him to New York, where he was to take a boat to Sweden. He became increasingly ill as he sped east and as he was getting back on the train in Cleveland he collapsed with a heart attack. He died two days later in a Cleveland hospital.

Harriet flew east and came back with the body. They buried Emil in Fargo. We children were considered too small to go to the funeral. Some time during the winter my Uncle Arnold boarded up the bunk house.

The next summer my father and I helped with the harvest—my father more than I. He had given up his previous job for selling insurance and that was going slowly so he came out to do the combining with my uncle. I rode back and forth in the wagons, went to fetch water, and at noon would ride the truck out to the fields, bouncing up and down alongside the lunches. I would sit on the running board of the pickup and eat with the men, drink out of the thermos, pull on my straw hat, and think of myself as a member of the crew.

Sometimes when they brought the wagons in to the granary I would jump up in the box and shovel grain alongside the men. There would be shiny black crickets popping up out of the flow of wheat, struggling to free themselves as they rushed toward the rattling chute. The shovel was oversized and felt as if it had been forged of lead. It wasn't long before my back began to ache, my eyes to sting with chaff. Around me the men worked fast, bodies glistening with sweat, but they kept on, making jokes about Give-'Em-Hell Harry and piano-playing Margaret and MacArthur's return. They laughed, kept shoveling, and talked about whether we'd go into Korea or not.

Harvest days were long and hard, going to sundown when it was necessary. At the end of the day I would sit at the pump and empty out my shoes, feet all prickly with chaff, and carefully wash arms, face, feet, and legs. The dog nosed all around me, curious, wondering why I didn't play any more. I'd ruff up his coat and then hobble stiffly to the house, half in imitation of the way I saw the men walk, half in dead earnest. The days passed, one like the other, and I couldn't imagine things ever being different.

Things were changing. A line of crackerbox houses had appeared on the horizon of the east pasture. When my grandfather had bought the farm it was nearly ten miles from town; the road had been dirt and a sudden spring rain could turn it into impassable mud. The city, however, kept growing. They paved the road and the rows of small identical houses kept moving closer. Even as we harvested, driving our old wooden wagons to the granary, the wind carried the sound of grunting bulldozers a mile or two away.

There was money to be made, no question. City men drove out to the farm to talk. There were discussions of zoning ordinances. My uncle, very quiet and gentle, became worried and taut. Some land was sold, at a good price; but the men still kept coming around.

That fall my father left to look for a job. When he returned he told us that we were moving to Wisconsin. He had a job at a munitions plant. They were hiring lots of men, at good pay, now that Korea had expanded into a war. My father was home for five or six days before he left again to start work. We were to follow as soon as the house was sold. He sent us letters full of funny drawings. It was the end of November before we left.

We spent Thanksgiving on the farm with Arnold and Harriet. Our father called us long-distance, his voice fuzzy and remote, and he had time for only a few words to each of us, all crowded around the phone.

Before dinner I took a walk with my uncle. Snow mixed with rain, pushed by a biting wind. In the east pasture the four remaining cattle huddled under a blasted willow, their back to the wind. Behind them in the distance was the row of tiny houses, their brash colors blunted by a curtain of snow. North Dakota winters managed to stop most construction.

"We'll get them in," my uncle said.

Together we circled the cattle, waving our arms, shooing them toward the gate. They were big animals and I kept my distance.

They straggled in, heads down, swaying heavily as they moved. Arnold unlatched the gate and pulled it back, the old wood creaking in the cold. The cows waited patiently.

"Ha-a-ay Bo-o-oss!" my uncle shouted, but they didn't move. I took a step forward, but one of the biggest animals swung his head toward me, staring balefully, head lowering. I froze. My first instinct was to run, but I held myself in place. It was snowing harder now. I wasn't going to be afraid. I wasn't going to be a child any more. In one sudden move I stepped up and whacked the animal on the flank. It let out a surprised moo and then lurched forward. A second animal scampered after it, slipping momentarily in the mud, sending up a spray of slush that spattered against my coat and face. The other animals moved quickly through.

My uncle locked the gate behind them, a bemused smile on his face. He wiped the slush off my face and my coat and gave me a soft cuff on the back of the neck.

Inside the house it was warm and noisy. The kitchen steamed with good, rich smells and my Aunt Harriet rushed back and forth setting the table. In the living room my little brother had just scattered the pieces of a puzzle my sisters were working on and they were all screeching at one another. My mother was arbitrating the fight, but it was only resolved when my aunt rang the big bell and it was time to sit down.

It was a fine dinner. The turkey was glistening brown and seemed arrogantly large. We fought over the drumsticks, my sister fed the dog under the table, and by the time the pumpkin pie came everybody was collapsed in their chairs.

After dinner I went upstairs by myself. The second floor was almost all unused space now. It had a peculiar, well-preserved air about it; an old Victrola that we sometimes cranked up, old paintings of misty seascapes or a stream tumbling through dark, shadowed woods. I went to the cabinet and hauled out the old photo albums. I leafed through, turned over the brittle pages carefully, past pictures of the horse-drawn threshers with their massive smoke-stacks, surrounded by huge crews of men, past snapshots of young men I didn't recognize dressed in odd uniforms, till I came to the picture I was looking for.

It was a picture of my father, my uncle and Emil taken many years before. The three of them were standing on an enormous snowdrift, so high their heads were at the same level as the telephone lines. Their arms were around one another, they leaned on their shovels, their chests thrown out, the road they had cleared far beneath them.

I had heard stories of the terrible blizzards and winter storms they had endured, but seeing the picture impressed me in an entirely different way. In the picture the figures were proud and smiling. Proud, certainly, for having conquered all that whiteness, shoveling for hours to clear a single, narrow track. Faces bitten by a wind that came down all the way from Canada without a single obstruction and that could blow up huge drifts, obliterating any trace of their work in a matter of minutes. Brilliantly white that snow must have been, stretching to the horizon in every direction, because in the picture their eyes squinted, unable to bear all that dazzling light. I sat for a long time with the gray yellow picture before me. Finally, hearing my sisters laughing and stumbling up the stairs, I quickly put the album back in its place and ran from the room.

We left the next day. We were taking an all-night train ride on the Milwaukee Road, making mail stops in a thousand small midwestern towns that had names like Cloquet, Mankato, St. Cloud, LaCrosse, Black River Falls, Tomah, Baraboo . . . . I had looked them up. My aunt and uncle drove us down to the station. It was four in the afternoon and already the sun was disappearing. A porter walked briskly across the empty platform pushing a rattling handtruck.

We climbed into the train and found seats. Harriet gave us surprise gifts, making us promise not to open them for at least an hour. Arnold stood in the aisle, saying nothing. He wore his gray suit and his old-fashioned black dress shoes that came up high on the ankle. I wondered what obligation had forced him to dress up when it made him so

36

obviously uncomfortable. I remembered Emil in his suit and how the strange clothes added to the awkwardness of parting.

It was stuffy in the compartment and Arnold tried to open a window which was jammed. He said something to a porter who shook his head mysteriously and walked on. The conductor gave a shout and it was time to go. Harriet gave us all quick hugs and then Arnold reached across to shake my hand, his big, callused brown hand sticking out of a starched white sleeve.

We stared out the frosted window into the darkening afternoon. Arnold and Harriet stood together on the platform. I saw Harriet wave. Clouds of white steam rose from under the wheels of the train and dispersed in the dark sky. Engulfed in drab, bulky winter clothes, the faces of my aunt and uncle seemed pale and small. The train groaned and jerked forward. They waved good-by and we waved back at them through the glass. The train began to move and it seemed that the station platform was carrying Arnold and Harriet away. We pressed to the glass, angling our faces against the window for the last possible look, but then there were only the dark shadows of buildings, the clattering sound as we crossed the bridge over the Red River, heading east to a new home.

That night on the train I couldn't sleep for a long time. My eyes stayed stubbornly open. I tried to see their faces, but couldn't. I tried to form their faces in my mind, one at a time, over and over, and failed each time. I stared at my brother and sisters curled asleep on seats around me. My mother sat quietly, watching me. Finally the monotonous clacking of rails put me to sleep and I rode all that night dreaming of being a Sioux brave, my shoulders pierced by leather thongs, hanging from a tall pole, staring up into the great sun.

Journal Entry—July 3

*Events occur that can change everything. I cannot
express in words what I feel, the emotions are too strong
and hit too hard on all sides. Nothing will ever be the same.
I do not want to go back, but where to go, what will
happen? Friday I slept with Daniel and it was good. It
came after a long, exhausting and involved conversation;
his love of Peter, his jealousy of Marilyn and the place she
is taking in Peter's life. He fears his own homosexuality
and wants, desires, women—me, in particular, now. He is
very restless and insecure, fearful of trusting anyone, but
more afraid of anyone trusting him. And we talked about
me, his shifting attitude toward me, my relationship to
Gene. We weighed, compared, tested, all the time drawing
closer to one another.*

 *After dinner we smoked. The high came on gradually, I
never felt out of control or really stoned. Daniel was
alternately animated and tense, like a wind-up doll, then
sad and very distant. His place is small, cluttered with
heaps of papers, books, projects. It was hot so we didn't
turn on the lights as it got dark. As we could see less and
less it seemed as if the noise from the street began to
penetrate his room; children shouting, a woman and man
fighting upstairs, bottles breaking in the alley. In the
darkness each voice, sound magnified, became more
powerful. At times Daniel talked a lot. I was drawn by his*

vulnerability, his need for someone to talk to. Yet whenever I start feeling older, wiser, motherly, he shakes me out of my smugness by his directness, by a look. More than anyone I've ever met he has the ability to ask for what he wants. We had toyed before. Now it was suddenly serious. When we touched there seemed no reason not to, it seemed natural, and not at all like a seduction. I can't explain what I feel now. Or what it is I want. Or even guess what it is that Daniel and I can be together.

The ball went to my brother on the other side of the court. He held the ball between his legs for a frozen second, waiting for me to commit myself, then broke quickly behind a solid pick. I tried to go through, but caught a shoulder in my chest. I went up desperately, but late, my brother was already up for the shot over my reaching hands. It banked off the board, feathered in.

"Shit," I mumbled.

Matt grinned.

My little brother wasn't little any more. He had flown to New York the week before, after his high school graduation. Meeting him at the airport had been a shock. In my wallet I carried a snapshot of a chipmunk-cheeked, freckle-faced kid. At the airport I met a tall, lean teenager who talked with a quick, edgy style, leaping from one thought to another, never completing any one. We were awkward with one another.

He brought a friend with him, Charles. Matt had written me that Charles was very intelligent, the valedictorian of the class. I could see why. His figure exuded organization. A neat young man, small, good posture, wispy blond hair, very serious, a firm Germanic handshake and an expensive camera draped around his neck. I did not find Charles a turn-on.

The playground was small, a narrow strip of asphalt sandwiched between high, dirty brick buildings and separated from the street by a high wire fence. There were fifteen to twenty spectators on the sidelines, mostly ballplayers. They leaned back on rickety folding chairs, bottles of soda between their feet, a couple of them staring balefully out from under towels. They joked, laughed, craned their necks to watch girls passing on the sidewalk. Charles sat stiffly among them, conspicuous in his painfully white tennis shoes.

I didn't hear anything but the thud of the ball, someone shouting out a pick, a hoarse yell for the shot. I saw only bodies twisting, feinting, moving, and the ball's quick flight back and forth, bounding and spinning. There was no time to think—of where Ann might be, or her afternoon with Daniel. I wiped the sweat from my eyes. On the court it was so simple. It came down to just wanting the ball.

The day after they arrived I had given them a tour of New York. It had been unsatisfactory for me, probably for them. Charles seemed to have a check list of things to see pinned up somewhere in his head. Whenever I tried to point out something not on his list I could almost hear windowshades rolling down inside his eyes. I made some not very funny jokes and perhaps some rather malicious ones about tourists and Brownie cameras. They had not been well taken.

Perhaps it was wrong to blame Charles. It wasn't his fault I wasn't able to talk to Matt. Matt was no longer a child, yet there was an old bond that I wanted to acknowledge, no, more than that; to reestablish. Yet every time I tried to speak I found that I was the one struggling with adolescent awkwardness.

I was irritated, too, by my own distraction. Matt would be talking and suddenly his words would strike something in me, triggering other, unuttered words, recalling a conversation with Ann, a half-remembered exchange, the pain and confusion of the last two months intruding on the present like the rap of a hammer on a darkened window, the shattering of glass. . . . Matt would stop talking, seeing my troubled face, wondering what he had said. I'd stare, try to cover up my absence with a joke.

They were leaving on Saturday. Friday I suggested that we play some ball. I was glad that I had. Matt was tough to play. There was nothing fancy about his game, but he was tall, strong and we battled even on the boards. I was pleased.

The game stayed close. We scored a basket to go up, 14–13. It was game point. Popo threw to Tommy. I went out to set a pick, but Lonnie was already through it. I moved to the basket, Tommy threw up a shot, a bad shot. Matt and I moved to the backboard together, banging for position, elbows digging in each other's chests. The shot bounded high off the back rim. I timed my leap, went up hard, Matt with me, bodies straining, twisting together. We hit the ball together, tipping it, backspinning the ball up into the air and this time it caught the rim as it came down, hung and dropped through.

The game was over. There was a lot of congratulatory hand-slapping, the ballplayers who had called next winners shuffled onto the court to warm up. I slouched toward the water fountain. There was a stiffness in my left calf I hadn't noticed before. I looked up at Matt.

"Mean man," I said.

He gave a mock scowl and we both laughed. I asked Popo for the time. It was a quarter of six. I had told Ann we would meet her at five-thirty to take Matt and Charles out to dinner.

"Hey, we better take off," I said. "We're late." I grabbed a handful of water from the fountain, wiped it, dripping, across my dirty sweating face.

When we got back to the apartment Ann wasn't there. I sat in the living room, unlacing my tennis shoes and talking to Charlie while Matt showered. We talked easily. Charlie didn't seem so bad . . . I laughed at myself.

The hot spray of the shower felt good. I closed my eyes and stood motionless, letting the water beat on the back of my neck, letting it pour down my body. The water was hot enough to raise goose bumps, but I didn't mind, the sting of the driving water gave a chilling pleasure. I felt the rising steam penetrate, working into the stiffening, tight muscles. I was jolted out of my reverie by the harsh, persistent ringing of the phone.

"I'll get it!" I shouted. I hopped out of the shower, grabbed a towel and stumbled to the phone, leaving a track of wet footprints across the floor. It was Ann.

"Hi."

"Hi."

"I tried to call you before."

"We were outside. Playing ball." I dried myself vigorously, pounded the water out of my ear. "Hey, where are you?"

"I'm still in East Harlem."

"Oh."

"Something has come up. I'm going to have dinner with Daniel." In the living room where Matt was getting dressed, they were laughing together. I turned, pressed closer to the phone.

"Wait a minute. I thought we said we were taking these guys out to dinner."

"It's important. I'm sorry. You can take them out, can't you?"

"Of course I can."

"Are you upset?"

"Does it matter?"

"Of course it does. Gene . . . ."

"I know. I'm being stupid."

"Don't worry. Please. All right?"

"I don't decide that."

"I know." Our conversation had become abrupt and awkward as if we were talking long-distance, expecting someone to cut in.

"I love you," she said. "You know that." She waited. "Don't you?"

"Yes."

"I won't be late."

"Bye."

"Bye."

I hung up. Charles was leafing through magazines, Matt was rearranging his suitcase. "Okay, you guys, enough of this locker room stuff." I snapped my towel at them. "Get dressed and let's get out of here."

We went to a Cuban food shop on 109th Street. It was

one of my favorite neighborhood restaurants. The food was cheap and good. The owner was a middle-aged Cuban who presided over the premises with constant smiles and nods. The only reminder of his lost past was a huge aerial photograph of pre-revolutionary Havana plastered on the wall over the counter.

It was the height of the dinner hour and the small restaurant was a swirl of activity. Waitresses in sheer pink dresses rushed back and forth. There was a jam of gawking people at the door, waiting for tables. Bright dishes of paella, pink seafood, steaming rice and beans slid by in every direction. From the row of red vinyl booths hands jabbed the air, syncopating the bursts of rapid-fire Spanish. The only points of stillness were the two or three pimps leaning against the counter in the front, nursing cups of coffee, cool and motionless in dark glasses and sharply cut suits.

The owner darted back and forth, hair flying as madly as any orchestra conductor's, arms waving, dropping a word to one person, then to another. He seemed to skate-board up and down the cafe, dishes clattering all around him, keeping everything just barely under control. The door to the kitchen opened every couple of minutes, issuing great puffs of steam which were punctuated by the red face of the beleaguered cook who would let out a yell like a sweaty Cuban tuba and slam the door shut again.

We ate. Charles was fascinated, eyes darting from one place to another. I attempted to joke, trying to keep up a flow of conversation, but I was forcing it, it wasn't working. I was out of sync. Charles didn't seen to notice, but Matt looked up. I felt he was waiting for me to speak.

I looked at him in a new way, trying to gauge him. What could I say to him? Why couldn't I speak to him? Perhaps it was an older brother's pride, refusing to admit any weakness, afraid to admit to any suggestion that my life was at least as confusing as his, that I had no handle on what was happening to me. Or perhaps there are certain things that can't be told. I felt my lips part to say something, but they closed again without uttering a sound; my eyes burned. I looked down.

The crunch of people pressed in on me. The crying of a child, the tinny sound of dropped silverware, hoarse laughter from another booth, the rattling maracas from the jukebox, all seemed discordant now. I asked for the check. We walked out into the dark street.

Matt and Charles decided they wanted to go on the Staten Island Ferry. I gave them a key and walked back to the apartment alone.

I tried to read but was too restless. I turned on the Mets, watched the game drift by, dreamlike under sharp arc lights, listening to Ralph Kiner drone on and on till I realized I didn't know who was pitching or what inning it was.

She hadn't said when she would be back. What she had said was simple enough. She was having dinner with Daniel. Period, end of thought. No, it wasn't the end of thought, either hers or mine. She would sleep with him. This time she would. And what would follow from that?

I leaned over and flipped channels. There was an old movie on Channel Five. A young, mustachioed Gary Cooper in *Lives of the Bengal Lancers*. British soldiers off in India fighting for the future of civilization in crisply starched uniforms.

I had met Daniel only once. That was early in the spring when Ann had him and the other two VISTAs she supervised over for dinner. They had been in the city for no more than a couple of months. They were anxious, lonely, going through the inevitable pains of making the transition from a college campus to life on First Avenue and 117th Street.

First impressions are difficult. It took half the evening to get names straight and begin to associate them with the few stories Ann had told me. I remember that the three seemed to be oddly shy around me. They deferred to me for no good reason, left long pauses after I had finished speaking, as if they were expecting more. I wondered what Ann had told them about me.

There was Bob Herron, a hardy, apple-cheeked midwestern boy who had just graduated from a small YMCA college in Illinois. He was friendly, easy, helped clear the dishes from the table without asking. He was the only one of the three I felt some measure of ease with. Peter was a graduate of Berkeley, wrote poetry, did, in fact, look like a student–poet; slight build, startling blue eyes, wire rim glasses, a soft voice, and delicate good looks. There also was something about him that resisted a quick summing up, a kind of reserve, a private self. I remembered something else Ann had told me about him. His father was a Mormon bishop in northern California and Peter had grown up in a strictly religious home. An incongruous bit of information. It didn't quite fit. We talked about writing and though he talked hesitantly, it seemed to me that he was genuinely bright.

As Peter talked, Daniel sat on the arm of a chair, one leg folded under him, smiling. He interrupted once to say something incomprehensible, creating an immediate and awkward silence. It didn't seem to bother him. He smiled and repeated what he had said. Ann skillfully guided the conversation on to other things.

Daniel made the strongest impression of the evening, hands down. He was physically small and somewhat awkward; with his long, dark curls, deep brown eyes and olive complexion there were moments when he bore a disturbing resemblance to Ann. I couldn't put a finger on exactly what made me uncomfortable: the hints at androgyny, his inability to understand the most self-evident statements, or his passive assurance that he would be tended to. He wasn't hostile; just naïve and without any interest in making accommodations with people. It may have been stupid to feel challenged, but I did; I felt as if I had made contact with someone truly alien to myself.

Whatever was strained in the evening, however, Ann handled beautifully. The respect they had for her was obvious. They looked to her for cues the way school-children look to a favorite teacher. She drew each of them out, one at a time, with a question, a smile, a laugh. I remember being proud of her, enjoying her. Everyone believed, finally, that we had created a lovely evening. At the end, sitting listening to music, drinking coffee, not saying anything, we had to tell them it was time to leave.

At the door Bob shook my hand, hemmed and hawed for a minute, then said, "It's nice to be in a home, you know?"

"Ya, I know," I said.

Gary Cooper and friends have been captured by the enemy. Not Cooper's fault, of course: the kid of the out-fit was messing with a beautiful woman spy. Their captor is a very rich, very polite maharajah who wants certain secret information. Cooper is strong and silent. The maharajah is upset, would be dismayed if he was forced into using exotic Oriental methods of torture. Cooper is not going to give in. He is taken to a table, his hands are strapped down. A quick shot of a pile of gleaming bamboo splints. The torturer is smiling. Will Cooper confess? No. The torturer picks up a splint. Tell us all you know. No. The camera shows only Cooper's face as the splints are driven deep beneath the nails, we see his face contort in agony, yet he is mute . . . .

I stare suddenly at my own hands, dark, stubbed shadows in the silver glow of the television. Even under torture would I confess? Would I know how, could I find a way to tell what had happened, what was happening?

I remember a friend telling me of the women who wove Oriental tapestry, how they grew their fingernails long and hard, then slit them and used them to hold the many-colored threads as they worked. How to weave a semblance of sense? Which threads to pick up? How to separate the true from the false?

Her attraction for them was perhaps simple. They were alone, displaced, she was a friend, a woman, she was sympathetic. It was Peter whom she found the most appealing of the three, who finally blurted out an abortive proposition and then quickly backed down in confusion and guilt. It was Ann who told me. Pick up then the thread of Peter and Daniel, their attraction for one another, long nights smoking and talking together, the relationship becoming more and more intense until it began to become frightening for both of them. Daniel willing to push it on further, daring to play it out, aware of touching Peter, Peter suddenly refusing to talk any more. Peter telling Daniel of his attraction for Ann, arousing a kind of jealousy in Daniel, forcing him to see her in a new way. Pick up then Peter abandoning both Ann and Daniel, moving in with a cheerful young blond who wore very short skirts and had wholesome attitudes and lived in the Village, leaving them both hurt in different ways.

Already I dislike what I'm beginning to weave. The analytic cast of it leaves a bad taste in my mouth. It is not merely geometry. There is much more than that. There is the memory of Ann and me using painful, hard, honest words, yet I can't remember half of those words, no sleight of hand will reproduce them. The one thing I am certain of is that all we did was done under the name of the love we had for one another. Does that arouse incredulous laughter? Let it. It is the only thing I will swear to. Beneath that, yes, were rougher, more frightening perceptions, my feeling a new hunger in her, watching her sudden swings of mood, seeing her standing naked in front of the mirror looking at her body as if she was watching a stranger.

What did she want? What did she want from them? I felt a growing fear, felt myself grabbing at her, trying to hold her, knowing that grasping only drove her further away.

Everything I remember raises more questions. My mind refuses, the pain begins to cut too deep, numbing, the weave collapses, the threads drop in a tangle.

My hands stiffened on the arms of the chair. I heard the elevator thump in the hallway. I waited, hoping it was her. It wasn't. I snapped off the set and sat in the dark.

Each time I heard the elevator I thought it was her. Each time it wasn't. Daniel had no phone, there was no way to call. I rubbed my eyes, trying to think. Without my glasses the darkness became a spider web, floating black nets spinning all around me, settling. I had to move, yet I waited.

When I was small and my parents went out at night I would lie awake in my bed until I heard the car pull into the garage. If it got too late I would begin to imagine catastrophes; a fire, an explosion, an automobile accident, their death. I stubbornly worked out all the consequences in my mind; the funeral, friends' sympathy, the splitting up of me and my brother and my sisters, our being sent away, orphaned. I would frighten myself finally with my morbidity and self-pity, but that didn't stop me.

Waiting for Ann brought it back, my imagination slipping back into old, forgotten patterns. It was late. She should be home. A robbery, an assault on the side streets of East Harlem. Who would notice? What if she was lying hurt somewhere? Fool. She was with Daniel. And that was safe, wasn't it? Flashes of anger alternated with rising panic. A man had been shot on the crosstown bus two nights before, over a wallet that contained three dollars. I wasn't a child, I couldn't lie in bed waiting. I would have to call hospitals and police stations, try to find her. I imagined her dead.

I heard the elevator and then steps. When she opened the door I was in the hall, waiting for her. Seeing her, all of my anger collapsed like a wall of loose brick.

She tilted her head, looking at me sadly. "Oh, God. I'm sorry." I took her hand. It was trembling. "Why did you wait? You should have gone with Matt. You shouldn't have waited."

"That's what I did. I couldn't help it."

She leaned over and kissed me. "It's so muggy out, God. I need a drink of water." She brushed by me on the way to the kitchen. "Where did Matt and Charles go?"

"The Statue of Liberty."

"Really?"

"Would I kid about the Statue of Liberty?"

"What time did they say they'd be back?"

"They didn't. They've probably been abducted by a band of mosquito-crazed Staten Islanders and we'll never see them again."

She laughed, then was serious. She leaned against the cabinet in the kitchen, reached up and stroked my face. "Please don't be upset. There's no reason. Honestly."

"Mmm."

"What were you thinking? Waiting here?"

"Lots of things. Some very strange things. Some not strange at all. I'm sure you know what they are."

She looked away. "Why don't we go out?" she said.

"Us?"

"Yes. Us."

"Where?"

"We'll go have ice cream. At Tom's. Hot fudge sundaes. Put quarters in the jukebox . . . ."

"Play 'Chantilly Lace.' "

"Exactly. You're reading my mind."

"What did you do?" I asked.

"At Daniel's? She looked at me. "We talked. Ate dinner. We smoked. He'd read this amazing . . . ."

"It's not a list I'm after. Did you sleep with him?" As soon as I asked the question I was ashamed.

"No." She answered quickly. Our eyes slid by one another, not quite catching. There was a silence, punctuated by a barely perceptible trembling as the subway passed far beneath us.

"I'm sorry that I asked," I said.

"No. Don't." She closed her eyes, biting the inside of her cheek. She shook her head. "Uh-uh."

We went out and had ice cream. She told me about her day. I didn't listen very carefully. It wasn't her fault. She had the ability to make good stories out of poverty program politics, Peewee baseball leagues in East Harlem, or the fact that Daniel was reading P. D. Ouspensky. What she said didn't matter. I was absorbed in the almost physical sensation of security. I was light-headed with a sense of relief. We were in a familiar place, doing a familiar thing.

I stopped her mid-sentence.

"Pour hot fudge on a Russian mystic and what d'ya get?"

"What?"

I smiled. "I don't know." She smiled. I reached across

and took her hand. She blushed, tightened her hand in mine.

We lay in bed motionless for a long time, not talking, neither of us asleep. I moved onto my side and put my hands on her shoulders, holding them there, and then ran my hands lightly down across her breasts and stomach. I repeated the motion. She turned slightly, the sheets rustling. She took my hands, kissed them, and we lay still together. We fell to sleep alone.

When I woke in the morning Ann stood in front of the mirror, brushing her hair. The sun streamed across the bed, danced in the mirror in bright, jagged points. Her hair was long, dark, smooth, and she brushed it with vigorous, almost angry, strokes.

"Hey," I said.

"Good morning."

"It's so early. What are you up for?"

"No reason."

"Oh ya?"

She put the brush down and turned to me. In the sun-filled room her face was suddenly dark with emotion. "I lied to you last night, Gene. I did sleep with him."

Did I move or not move? What did my face show? All I remember is that I did not say anything.

"Say something," she said. "Please. It's too important not to say anything."

"Why didn't you tell me last night?"

"I don't know. I couldn't."

I was chilled, unbelieving. I struggled to understand that things were different. Things were the same. It was morning, the sun streamed across the bed, danced in the mirror, her hairbrush rested on the heavy, carved wooden chest, the book she had been reading for three weeks lay open on the night stand, I lay half-wrapped in blankets.

Still she stood in front of me, her thin childish arms dropped to her side, leaving her vulnerable, exposed, her long, dark hair falling down over olive shoulders, across the small, soft breasts of a girl. She trembled, held herself from crying, yet not backing down. She was very brave. Her silence insisted. Things were changed. She was not to cry. Or lie. Again. Things were changed. My mind could not get around it.

"I don't know what to say," I said. "I don't know . . . ." She turned suddenly, her face half-hidden by a curtain of hair, yet I saw that she was afraid. "Do you know what I wish?" I said.

"What?"

"Shit. I wish I knew a way to pull you back to me."

She sat down on the bed, put her hand on my neck. When she spoke it was slowly, softly, murmuring half to herself. "It doesn't mean that I'm not with you. I'm here. I'm with you. I want to be here."

My body twisted away from her under the covers. I put my head down into the pillow, a child's escape. "I know, I know . . . ." I said.

"I love you, Gene."

"Goddamn it, Ann!" My curse was without any force, like an arrow shot into deep water. I heard someone move in the other room. With a shock I remembered Matt and Charles sleeping there. I smiled. "No time to make a scene, is it? Two teenagers in the living room. Nice timing. You're safe."

"No, I'm not," she said.

I grabbed her face, turned it to mine, making her look at me. We stared into each other's eyes without flinching. I thought I knew how to read the soft, trusting weight of those eyes. Now I wasn't sure. I let my hand fall from her face.

"What time are we supposed to drive them to the airport?" Ann asked.

"They should be there by eleven. We'd better get them up."

We borrowed Ann's parents' car to take the two boys to Kennedy. No one talked much on the drive out.

At the boarding gate there was a mass of people. Ann stood alone at the observation window, watching planes struggle heavily into the smog-brightened air. Matt and Charles' plane finally crawled into position, brisk technicians scurrying under the blowing, whining machine. I shook hands with Matt. I gave Charles a whack on the back. They moved toward the gate, moving into the stream of travelers. Matt looked back, smiled, said something that I missed. I waved good-by and they were gone.

A gate or two away a flight had just come in and the crowd jammed the hallway. We tried to sidestep our way around them. People were smiling, hugging, kissing, greeting one another. A middle-aged woman in a gaudy red suit let out a shriek, dropped all her packages and ran to embrace a grinning sister, friend, something. Together Ann and I walked back up the long, shiny hallway, making our way through streams of people hugging suitcases, gifts crooked under their arms. Silently we passed them, catching bits of stories, snatches of conversation.

It was a hot day, traffic was heavy going back into the city. I turned on the radio, filling the car with the incessant noise of WABC. I wove slowly in and out of traffic on the Triboro. A car was stalled in the middle lane and everyone had to inch around him. The driver stood stranded in the road, his cheeks puffed out in disgust. Seen through the black guy wires and beams of the bridge the city skyline shimmered like a dirty mirage.

"Talk," Ann said.

"Mmm . . . ." I said, the sound of a person who doesn't want to be wakened.

"Please."

I blurted the words out. "Was it good?"

"Yes," she said.

The traffic speeded up again. I started passing trucks, bumping over a rutted section of the road. Battered, twisted roadsigns lined the bridge like sentinels, wrenched and useless as words.

We said nothing more. I swung the car down off the Triboro, down onto 125th Street, moving slowly, edging for position on the crowded, noisy streets. My eyes moved quickly, silently, watching for children darting out suddenly between the cars.

I set down her suitcases momentarily so that I could open the door. She hesitated, looked back as if remembering something. The final unattended detail, the squat black seaman's chest with its gleaming brass locks, sat heavily as a sullen animal in the middle of the living room floor.

"Sure," I said. "It's no problem."

"You'll tell the Railway Express people . . . ."

She wore a soft new dress. Her hair, dark and clean, curled at her shoulders. She looked as fresh as a little girl. I felt a pull back to her that I was afraid to acknowledge, that I wanted to fight. I took her hand, playing her fingertips lightly against my own.

"You'll come down with me, won't you?" she said.

"Of course. We'll get you a cab." I picked up the suit-cases again. "I'd rather not ride all the way out to the airport with you. Is that all right?"

"That's all right."

"Let's go then."

"Gene . . . ."

"Come on." I was irritated, I wanted to leave.

"I'm sorry," she said.

"Please don't say anything . . . ." She leaned to me, put her arms around my waist. She let her head rest against my chest. I started to kiss her, hard, held her, and suddenly I was murmuring desperate, automatic words, "It will be all right, it will be all right . . . ."

A reconciliation with Gene, yet a realization that we must go on in a new way. Tuesday Peter and Marilyn came over and it was awkward because Daniel had told them he was sleeping with me. We couldn't really talk about it, but it was in the air. The wounds are still too fresh.

I swung the suitcases through the door and was in the hallway when I realized that she hadn't moved. She stood stock-still, crying. I turned on her, frantic, please stop, there's nothing to be done about it, not now, it's been decided . . . . We took the stairs down, avoiding the elevator. We slipped out of the building as if we were fleeing.

As we hit the street, the sun stunned our eyes. Banks of snow gleamed as they melted in the sudden January warmth. A stiff old Chinese man stood on the curb, staring incredulously at the slush running in the gutters. Ann and I saw him together, smiled together, saying nothing. She held my arm. I felt the smallness of her hand on my elbow.

She waited while I went into the street to flag down a cab. I held up a hand. Traffic whizzing by sent up sheets of water. I was angry now, angry at the final, useless rush of emotion I felt for her. I jerked my hand higher, waving.

Daniel upset when we saw him after the Ian and Sylvia concert and did not talk. It was G and D's first meeting since Gene has known. I felt terrible after it because I wanted to talk to Daniel, to let it be unforced. Then when he called I was overjoyed. Gene sensed it. Oh, my physical passion for Daniel is not entirely over yet, but being with him frees me in so many other ways.

A taxi swerved across two lanes of traffic, weaving like a motorboat. I grabbed for her bags and we ran for it. I swung the suitcases into the front seat.

"I'll call you," she said. "In a day or two. As soon as I get settled."

"Okay."

"You getting in or not?" It was the cabbie leaning across the front seat.

She slipped down into the cab. She reached out and caught my hand. I felt shy suddenly. I bent over and kissed her.

"Okay, babe. I love you," I said.

"I love you too," she said. The words I wanted, but wrong somehow, they had to be wrong. I shut the door. The cab pulled away. I stood watching, waiting to see if she would turn to look back, but there were only reflections of high buildings sliding across the curved window of the taxi, and the glare of sunlight.

I am unsure of most everything now, only somehow I manage a facade of stability and confidence—at least on the job and with not-so-close friends. Gene, too, perhaps a bit

*more preoccupied at times, but in general as easygoing and
funny as usual. And it is not that way at all.*

*Daniel slept over Tues. night because of the riots in
E. Harlem, stayed Wens. morning and I spent it talking
with him, he called Thurs. night and came over Friday.
Gene finally laid down an ultimatum. "I don't want you to
see him again." He thinks Daniel is brazen and knows
exactly what he is doing. Gene is jealous and feels terrible
when I see Daniel. My first reaction was to run away, then
to cry. I just had hoped things could continue with Daniel
until they reached their natural end. As I think they will.
Daniel makes me a person I can be with no other. I love
Gene, I know I do, but I need other people too.*

I stared up at our apartment windows. I wasn't going
back there. Not yet. What to do then? Anything. I wandered down Broadway, bought a paper, read the Larry
Merchant column on the Knicks, caught a subway downtown.

I moved by the dance halls, movie theaters, curio shops
with their shrunken heads, pennants, t-shirts, plasti-obscene
Jesuses who rolled their eyes heavenward as I passed. When
I was tired of walking I went into a hero sandwich shop. I
sat in the corner and watched high-school students laughing and flirting. The jukebox was on as high as it would go.

*We are going to California next month for a vacation.
We decided together and it is what we want to do. It is
crazy in some ways but I want an adventure right now and I
am restless to move.*

*Everything is subject to change. Gene and I are together,
as strongly as we have ever been, and yet Daniel is included.
I don't think anyone could understand. There is no fooling*

myself that he is just a friend. He is something of everything. Gene knows this and it is painful to him . . . yet I can't lie to him.

The afternoon had turned dark by the time I left the restaurant and for a second I wasn't sure where I was. I went to a phone and tried to call several friends, but it was still too early for anyone to be back from work. I started walking. The blinking lights on the skin flick marquees throbbed red as a wound. It was impossible to believe that she was gone.

Daniel on my mind. He went to Hartford to see a friend who tried to seduce him back into homosexuality. He had a traumatic time and came back Sat. as low as I've ever seen him. Yet he looks for the bizarre. He seeks it out. We talked for three hours and on Sunday the three of us went to the movies. Jules, Jim, and Kate. Wrong. Analogies are too easy. Whatever is pulling me is too strong for me to objectively and rationally say no. It was obvious Sat. night that the bond between D. and me was so strong that if G. had not been here we would have become lovers again— more serious and dangerous than that short exploratory affair of two months ago. I feel completely caught and willing to let Daniel make the decisions in relation to us.

There are no trustworthy records of what happened that summer and fall. Now it seems all a tangle of contradictory impressions. I remember the immediate, deadening shock when she told me she had slept with him, the new, bitter taste of jealousy, but I remember we seemed to draw closer together for a time.

I remember a Sunday afternoon sitting in Riverside Park, the Sunday *Times* between us. It was a warm day and around us were sandboxes jammed with shovel-waving three-year-olds, benches of stiff-backed bookreaders and curled-up winos, plus a constant parade of Puerto Rican softball players, parents dragging tricycles, and dogwalkers. I folded up the *Travel and Resorts* section and sat watching her until she finally became aware of me and looked up.

"What are you doing?"

"Looking at your face."

"What for?"

"Trying to memorize it . . . ."

She laughed. "I'm the one with the two eyes, one nose . . . ."

"And the new lover," I said. She was silent. "I'm sorry. It's just that for a long time I've thought of you as being a part of me . . . . As if we had blurred together. Now the images are getting a lot sharper."

"That's not bad then."

"Maybe not. You know what?"

"What?"

"I prize you."

"Prize me?"

"That's right. I prize you."

She leaned over and kissed me.

"I still want you with me."

"I'm with you now."

"What will happen to us?"

"I don't know."

"When you saw Daniel . . . ."

"Daniel has nothing to do with it."

"Daniel has a lot to do with it. If you spent all day Friday with him . . . ."

"Gene, what matters to us is the time that we're together.

Isn't it? Right now matters. And isn't it nice? And isn't it even lovely?"

"Sure."

We got up to leave, arm in arm. There was soft sunlight through the trees and an old lady smiled up at us as if we were teenage lovers.

Over that summer I listened to her: I won't sleep with him again, it's too dangerous, I don't want to hurt you, but I have to see him again. I need him, he makes me alive, my life has been a long straight line and I'm going to change that. He needs me, I help him, it isn't basically sexual. I've never known anyone like him. Just because we're married doesn't mean we're each other's property. It's possible to love more than one person, you've admitted it yourself. I care for him in a different way than I care for you.

Where to find a rule? There was no rule.

Over that summer I watched her, watched her change, and I waited for her. She lost weight, slipped under a hundred pounds. She became almost doll-like, but there was a hunger about her, she was consciously sexual for the first time. On the street people looked at her differently, as if a lens had been adjusted. She bought new, bright clothes. Look at me, I'm changing . . . .

Where to find a rule? There was no rule.

Once he called her up and said he had to see her. He was desperate. She said he could come over. I told her I couldn't stay. I went out, saw a film, trying to give her room, trying to be fair, yet I imagined him touching her and I hated it, hated him, wanted to kick in his face.

There was no rule. Except the rule of our own honesty. We clung to honesty the way a drowning man clings to a piece of driftwood. If we were honest, if we didn't lie, if we said it, no matter how painful, things would work out. If I hadn't read her journal I might have gone on believing that.

And so we slept together again. Partly because of a need for sexual relief from the tremendous emotional and physical desire we both felt over the weekend and which returned when we saw one another. I did not feel guilty or that it was a big thing. We talked again on Friday. Daniel again denying certain feelings but they are there. Daniel has a hard time listening—admits he gets caught up in the sensual aspect of the conversation. He is afraid to open himself up for too long a time and then he pulls the door shut. Now he is off to California, to home, in a hope that it will make a difference in his dissatisfactions. He'll be gone for about a month. We made no definite plans to see each other there. He can't be held to specifics. It's okay.

Gene very upset with the realization that I give Daniel certain priorities. We discussed the possibility of some kind of separation. Gene very upset at first, can't understand that I say it's more than just Daniel. Perhaps I should get away from both of them. I am being lost to Gene slowly. I try to come back, but cannot.

Though she never asked me she must have guessed that I read it. Several times I came close to telling her but never did. I was ashamed. She must have known. There were days when the journal was mysteriously missing or moved from its usual position in the bedside table. I was careful never to mention things I could have known only from the journal, yet there were other ways to use it, to dig at her, force her into the corner, force her to lie.

She had kept diaries off and on since her childhood. Once she had shown me an old diary with a red leather cover, initialed in gold, with a tiny lock shaped like a heart. It was full of brave resolutions to work harder, to be kinder, lists of birthday party guests, reports of state fairs and summer camps. Between the pages we found crumbly remains of grass plucked from the lawn of a one-time boyfriend. We blew the ancient brown leaves into the wastebasket and laughed.

In the spring she began to write in her journal regularly again. The journal took on a new importance. There were so many changes in her that she wanted a way to release them, to verify them, to reconstruct them. After dinner she would sit at the desk, disciplined as any Latin student, and write for as long as an hour at a time without interruption.

Many times before in our marriage it had occurred to me to read her journal, and it had always seemed harmless. The main deterrent was the feeling that reading another person's journal was one of the meaner and more humiliating sins, ranking with getting caught with your hand in the cookie jar or Peeping-Tomism. As the spring went on and she became more deeply involved with Daniel the temptation grew and became more dangerous.

I began to read it, carefully removing whatever else was in the drawer so that I could be sure to replace the journal in its precise spot. I would lie on the bed and read, listening for the door. Several times I vowed not to look at it again, but as summer came there were more opportunities, more times when I was alone, waiting for her to return.

It may have been punishing and degrading to go on reading, but I grew to depend on the journal. It was something to hold on to, a record, a blindman's cane for tapping across unfamiliar ground, a mirror.

A mirror not intended for me, perhaps, but giving a harsh, clear reflection, as merciless as the queen's looking glass in Snow White. It was valuable precisely because it took no account of me, because she wrote only for herself without softening anything out of pity. The second time she slept with Daniel, she didn't tell me. The journal did. But was it true? Any truer than what she told me? No truer than a fun-house mirror with its rolling distortions. It told its own lies. Over and over in the journal she said that she was growing freer of Daniel, the relationship was finding its own natural end, that sexuality had little or nothing to do with it. That she could love more than one person and lose none.

Perhaps I should have found a way to answer her, perhaps I should have written in the margins, made neat red-pencil corrections. But no amount of corrections could have changed what happened. As we drifted apart, reading the journal became like reading a report from a stranger. The same things did not happen to us. Again as in a mirror, everything was inverted, the left hand became the right; when she was with him and happy, I was alone and waiting. What made her joyous and full of a new, driving energy was terror and loss for me. I woke up every morning hoping that all the madness would fall away and that things would be as they had been before. She never looked back. Whatever happened later, early in that summer she was free, strong, liberated, desired. Beautiful. She was in love. With her new-found power. With Daniel. And with me. It would be easier to believe that she didn't care for me then, but she did. She never tried to be vicious, and even to the end, when it became confusing, hard, insane, she tried to love me.

I want to be with someone, to have an intimate relationship. Daniel probably too scared. I wonder where he is and what he is doing. I wonder that every day. Emotionally he fills my time.Why? I feel so little passion, so little closeness to Gene, and yet it is he who really loves

me, cares, gives and does not hurt me. Yet I would be
Daniel's lover and live with him if he desired it.

We flew to Los Angeles on the first of September for a
vacation, knowing that Daniel was there and that we would
probably see him. Looking back I can think of no satis-
factory reason why I could have agreed to go. She was sure
he would be in San Francisco by the time that we arrived,
we needed to get out of New York, there were relatives to
visit, what a gas to do Disneyland and Knotts Berry Farm
and bikers, beaches, movie stars, the whole L.A. scene . . . .
It sounds so flimsy to me now, trying to write it down. It
didn't then. Ann had the power to make the most astonish-
ing proposal sound sane and normal, even the two of us
flying across the country to meet her lover.

Why did I let it happen? Because I craved punishment.
Because I was weak. Because I wanted to play it out all the
way. I wanted to see what would happen. Because I loved
her and still believed things could again be what they had
been once. Trying to guess at my motives now is like throwing darts blindfolded.

We were sitting by a pool when she told me she was
going over to see if Daniel was home. "You don't have to
come with me," she said.

"Goddamn, Ann."

"Just give me the keys then." She extended a hand.

Sun glinted off the unnaturally blue water. The pool was
at the center of a pink stucco apartment complex. Deck
chairs spoked the pool and fifty- and sixty-year-old widows
lay back, staring into a bright, cloudless sky, sucking up
health, their deep tans masking any traces of grief.

"Tell me how come?"

"How come what?"

"How come every time it gets down to a choice between Daniel and me, you choose Daniel?"

She was silent for a moment. "I want to see him. Isn't that simple enough?"

"I don't want you to go. Please. There's no reason."

"Except that I want to see him. I can do what I want. Didn't you say that? Didn't we agree?" She stopped. "It won't be for long. It will be fine. We can make it be whatever we want it to be. We'll all be friends. It can be easy . . . ."

I drove her. Daniel lived in Hollywood. We passed through palm-shaded streets, low Spanish houses with red tile roofs. I parked across the street. "You go see if he's there," I said. I watched as she dashed into the house. I didn't see who answered the door.

Ten, fifteen minutes passed. I thought of going to the door, but wasn't able to. I listened to the car radio. It was hot. I stared at a middle-aged man watering his lawn. He moved slowly across the sun-brilliant grass, the coils of hose unfurling behind him. I thought of her. I thought of Daniel. I thought of them together inside. The exteriors of the houses baked silently in the sun, the flowers were bright and still as if they had been painted.

I hit the horn. Once. Twice. Then harder. I saw the man stop, look up from his lawn. Two women coming up the walk shied away suddenly. I shut them out. I leaned against the horn, drove my head against the metal rim, letting the sound pierce the quiet afternoon, held it till the horn began to waver like a scream. Ann appeared suddenly at the door and came running out to me.

She threw open the car door. "What's wrong?" There was panic in her voice. I didn't look up; the horn had stopped, but my hands were still frozen on the steering wheel. "Nothing happened. He wasn't even there, Gene.

He's still in San Francisco. It was just his parents. That was all. His parents." She reached across and put her hand over mine, working the fingers free from the wheel; I could feel her hand trembling.

I cannot let D. enslave me this way. I have to leave NY, find something by myself. I cannot realize what Gene means to me, to my life, unless I separate myself from him.

I want to run away, but cannot. Each week is such turmoil because there is no consistency to him. D. says, "Consistency is a trick we play on one another." I live in complete uncertainty as to what will happen next with us. Daniel was at the bottom when we came back from the weekend in Philadelphia. He spent too much time thinking about us and hadn't wanted me to go. We talked about how hard it had become, yet how impossible it is to break away. How he cares, how he doesn't. And I felt I must let him decide, because I cannot cut it off. I will not force him.

"One . . . Two . . . Three . . . Four . . . we're gonna stop this fuckin' war!" Helicopters buzzed overhead like whirring halos in the autumn sky. It had been a long hard day; Ann was exhausted from marching; but as we crossed over the bridge into Virginia with thousands of others, songs and chants flowing back and forth through the marchers, it was hard to be cynical. This time, this demonstration, we were going to have an effect. "All we are asking . . . ."

Daniel was there, too, somewhere. We had made no plans to meet him. Enough time had been spent on Daniel. In her journal Ann had talked about opening up the new experience: instead, everything seemed to be narrowing to a single, solipsistic point. Her affair with Daniel had dominated all other aspects of our life. I had insisted that Ann and I go to the march on the Pentagon together; there were things in the world more serious than her and Daniel's self-expression; the war was one of them.

It was late afternoon by the time we reached the Pentagon parking lot. The rally was over and all the speakers had left. People were climbing aboard the Women's Strike for Peace buses.

The Pentagon lay beyond a shrubbed embankment. We stood with a group of our friends trying to decide what to do next. No one really wanted to turn around and walk back. Make a run on the Pentagon . . . no one was sure they were ready to be arrested and no one wanted to cop out on their friends.

"Aww, come on," I said. "This is stupid. We come all this way to hang around the parking lot? What are they gonna do to us? We'll just go look." Ann leaned against me, too tired to speak. "We can decide up there. All right?" No one said anything. "All right?"

We climbed up the slope and bent low to make our way through the bushes. Crushed together on the far side of the bushes was a crowd of a hundred demonstrators, face to face with a line of soldiers.

We were jammed so close together it was hard to move, or even to see. Someone started a chant: "Join us, join us . . . ." Kids were hanging from the trees. Beyond the line of soldiers lay the green sloping lawns of the Pentagon, immaculate and bright as a golf course, and every few minutes someone would dash across, outsprinting the military and everyone would cheer. I was excited by it. I took Ann's hand and pushed further into the crowd.

A freaked-out bandanaed Jesus stood in front of a black soldier, throwing flowers in the soldier's face, harder and harder, shouting, "Join us, join us . . . ." A jeep of officers bumped across the lawn toward us.

I realized suddenly that I had lost Ann's hand. I looked

back; she was no more than five yards from me, but turned away and staring through the crowd. I followed her gaze to a slightly built young man in a blue windbreaker. I felt a leap of panic at the dark curls, the olive complexion, the familiar gesture of the hands jammed deep in the pockets; but then he turned and I could see his face. It was not Daniel.

"It's not him," I said. Ann looked up at me.

"I didn't think it was," she said.

"Then what were you thinking?"

"I wasn't thinking anything." She said something more, but I couldn't hear it; her words were drowned out by the shouts of the people around us. We looked up. A kid had dashed through the line of soldiers and was sprinting across the green lawn. Two or three soldiers ran after him, but he dodged them like a swivel-hipped halfback. Hoarse cheers and applause went up. After a couple hundred yards when no one was chasing him, he slowed to a walk, a small figure looking back at us from an immense grassy slope, uncertain, now, where he was to run to.

"I've had enough," I said. "Let's go."

Thurs. night he called and conversation was good, very good and I saw him again Friday. A crazy day—too much to absorb all at once and I am still reeling from it. We were on the same wavelength and after initial nervousness broke through to talk openly about our fears and loneliness and what limits we want to impose on our relationship, but cannot. Daniel trying to be detached, to look for comfortable, easy relationships—yet these are not for him. Sex more ecstatic for him in fantasy and alone than the real thing. Why? He is so afraid to give.

We took pictures, went to his place. I practiced the guitar, he shaved and took a bath. "Oh, let's lie down

naked together and relax." "But it will lead to sex and I
disappoint you and you can't relax unless you are high and
you are really afraid of sex with me."

But we smoked, not much, just enough to feel it. We
looked at each other's bodies and the sex came. I learned
from it—we are not there yet, but when he kisses and sucks
my breasts my femaleness overcomes me and it is the
greatest pleasure in itself. Ah, but work for him.

Then we laughed and came home together for a dinner
with Gene. How could we? I was afraid, but after the initial
awkwardness and Gene's hostility, it worked. Was it crazy?
Nothing's crazy if it works.

I came home at five. I had spent half the afternoon in a
producer's office, smiling at his secretary. In the end I de-
posited a script and left. It felt a little like dropping it down
a well, but at least I had done it defiantly.

Ann was already home by the time I got back. When I
walked into the bedroom there was half a second when I
wasn't sure what had changed.

"Do you like it?"

Locks of her dark hair lay curled on the bureau. She had
the scissors in her hand.

"Oh, my God . . . ."

"Well?"

"I don't know. It's the young Jean Seberg look."

Her face screwed up in annoyance. "I was tired of all that
hair. It was getting so long it was getting heavy and hot . . . .
I like it," she said fiercely.

I sat down on the bed. Picking up the scissors, I opened
them and held them under my nose like a silver mustache.
She smiled. "If it's all right with you, it's all right with me,"
I said. "How was your day?"

"All right."

"What did you do?"

"I went to boring meetings all morning. Human Resources . . . talk about a misnomer. Then I checked out to the field and met Daniel downtown. We rummaged around the Strand for old books."

"Oh."

"Have you ever heard of Edgar Cayce? Daniel's been reading him. It's fantastic. He's this prophet from West Virginia or someplace . . . ."

"I've heard of Edgar Cayce. It's a bunch of sophomoric bullshit."

She ignored what I was saying. She touched her hair, staring into the mirror, smiling at the reflection of her new self. The two of them smiled in complicity, hiding their secret from me.

It has opened up now—D. and I talked. He is lonely and insecure and afraid of all the craziness he lives in. "Let us see if we can make the craziness of our involvement more natural." Sunday he came over. The three of us talked until 2 A.M. I could not believe that we could be there, expressing feelings as openly as we did. I was afraid at first, but in the end I felt a great responsibility lifted from my shoulders— I do not have to play mediator any more. Daniel saying, "I'm twenty years old. I want to have twenty-year-old relationships. I want things to be easier, simpler. I want to ride around in cars and pick up girls . . . . It's all gotten too heavy . . . ." Yet finally he said, "Wherever I go, if you are there, I would come and see you. That is the way the relationship is. I would want to be with you." There are others in his life like that too, but it doesn't matter.

It looks as if the relationship will have a natural end— he will be leaving in January—going back to school—San Francisco State. I love him. I do not doubt he knows it—

*it is not wrong, but the drive to possess him, to want him
for myself, the feelings of jealousy—so now I know what
Gene feels about me. We've come full circle—but I must
free myself from that.*

"What if we saw someone?"

"Saw someone?"

"Ya. A marriage counselor. Somebody."

"A shrink? I thought you didn't approve of that sort of
thing."

"Maybe I didn't."

"You think one of us is crazy?"

"I think that if we're going to work this thing out we
need help. Don't we?"

Her tone softened. "There are a couple of problems."

"What?"

"For one, both people have to be committed . . . ."

"To staying and working it out. And you're not sure that
you are."

"Be fair."

"What's unfair about that? He's going to California and
you're chasing after him."

"I am not."

"What are you going out there for, the weather?"

"That's right. For the weather. For sunshine and warmth
and a chance to live exactly as I choose for once in my life."

"What do you mean? Last week you were going to buy a
car and drive out together."

"It would have been cheaper."

"He's got you, you know that? He's got you in a corner."

"How many times do I have to tell you that Daniel isn't
the main issue?"

"Do you think that going to L.A. is going to solve anything? Anything at all?"

74

"He'll be in San Francisco. I may not see him at all . . . ."
There was no point in arguing stupidly. "I don't want to lose you," I said. "That's all."
"I wouldn't be good with a therapist. It's much harder when you know all the tricks. It gets too . . . too conscious. I think I could probably convince them of whatever I wanted to."
"I don't think you're quite that good."
"I do."

The most unbelievable, blurry weekend. Now getting clearer. G. went to Montreal, just to get away. I didn't hear from Daniel, went lower and lower. I ended up staying with Bob Friday night. Why? Attempt to break away from Daniel. "You are not the only other man I have slept with," and to show Gene that sex is not the major part of my relationship with D., to diminish it by having sex with someone else. I'm sure there were other motives too—but it was too crazy and I felt guilty using Bob—as if I was a female Daniel. Why? No physical attraction, no real desire. Bob is not a particularly sexual person. But it was done. We had a long talk and I apologized. A scene of bewilderment. Saturday we met Daniel and Peter. Oh, yes, Peter is beautiful and without Marilyn the same. We talked for several hours. Bob left. I was relieved. I stayed with Daniel and told him what happened. He pulled some of it out of me, but without any real rejection on his part. He was going out with Abigail, but said I could stay at his place. Then it happened, that overwhelming, physical, sensual closeness, sex as I've never known it. Vince came in and broke the spell. Vince, Daniel's new roommate, sick, addicted, sad. Daniel went off to Abigail and a party. I helped Vince get ready for work. He was stoned on three bags of heroin. I had to help him wash and dress himself. A

75

very sick person with the classic homosexual problem, which he insists on denying. He lived with his mother in East Harlem all his life, until he moved in with Daniel. Works at a dead-end job in the garment district. Such a sad person. Daniel came home at one-thirty and played the guitar for a while—then we slept. Sunday was quiet. I came home at one or so, by myself. I felt I'd been through so much intensity that I could not go on.

I awoke, sensing something wrong, but confused in the darkness. I felt the delicate trembling of the bed. She was beside me. I felt her moving. I spun on her.
"What are you doing?"
"Nothing."
Her face was turned away from me. The room was dark and close. I reached down under the twisted blankets to touch her. She was still, her arm rigid, reaching down between her legs.
"Stop it," I said. "Please, come here . . . ." I turned her face to me. "With me. With me."
"No."
"Then stop."
"I was restless. I couldn't sleep."
"I don't care, I want you to stop!" My own rage frightened me, paralyzed me. I wanted to hit her, hard, but if I did I would hurt her. I didn't do anything.
She slipped out of bed, a pale shadow in the doorway. I heard her walk into the living room. I lay listening to the street noises. I was awake when she returned to bed. I didn't try to touch her.

Our anniversary, the fourth, and yet we both know it may be the last. We are too far apart to be married, though close in other ways. I am going again—to L.A. in mid-

January, and maybe Gene will come to visit in the spring and we will make some final decision then. Sometimes I feel so strong about it—sometimes weak—I cannot believe it when I come out of feeling so low, so depressed, so like crying. I try to remember that it does not go on forever and that I do have times of peacefulness and inner strength. Gene, too, only he fools me because I think he is all right and that we have settled certain things and then something sets him off—and it scares me what happens to him—how deeply he retreats inside himself. It makes me realize all the more that our plans for separation will not be easy.

She came through the door at five-thirty and she was high. Not reeling drunk, but smiling and flip and completely at ease. It pissed me off.

"So what have you been drinking?"

"How could you tell?"

"How could I not tell?"

"Frozen daiquiris. A fine tropical drink." She leafed through the mail. "We didn't get the Macy's bill?"

"Fuck Macy's. What are you getting drunk for?"

"What for? For lunch."

"With who?"

"With whom. I thought you were a writer."

"I asked you a question."

"Am I under oath?"

"No."

"Wilkinson."

"Oh, God."

"Oh, God, what?"

"Oh, God, nothing."

"You're looking very sour," she said.

I probably did. I should have laughed. It was funny. Al Wilkinson was the recreation director for one of the biggest settlement houses in East Harlem. Also a self-proclaimed stud. There were plenty of anecdotes about Wilkinson's Underground Railroad that ran young girls uptown from the Columbia School of Social Work, Neighborhood Youth Corps, VISTA and other sectors of the War on Poverty. It was ridiculous. It made me furious.

"I thought you did better than that," I said.

"I did nothing. He took me out to lunch."

"That's cool."

"It's part of my job, right?"

"That's cool."

"Stop being stupid! There's no reason for you to get...."

"Did he proposition you or not?" My question stopped her long enough to make me push on. "Did he?"

"Nothing happened."

"What about our fabled honesty?"

"Yes, he propositioned me."

"How come? Why do you . . . . Haven't you proved about all there is to prove?"

Her voice rose in self-defense. "It was silly. How you can get so paranoid . . . . It was a game. Have you ever played a game? You do it for the fun of it. He thought he was so smooth . . . . You would have laughed at him. It was nothing. Absolutely nothing."

"But you got drunk?"

"The drinks were good."

"Ya?"

"Ya. And he asked me for a date."

"You dig telling me this stuff, right?"

"I don't tell you anything you don't want to hear." She saw me stiffen and her voice changed. "I told him no. I said I was very involved with my husband. He said he understood that."

"That was big of him."

She looked at me. "I don't want to fight."

I was sober and I did want to fight. About a lot more than Wilkinson. About the fact that she had slept with Bob, a stupid, pointless seduction, and she had lied to me about it. I knew, I had read it in the journal, yet I wasn't supposed to know, therefore I couldn't be angry. It had become progressively more insane, more degrading. I knew that she had slept with Bob again, after the first time that had been so terrible by her own admission. Why? To show Daniel something, or me. I didn't know. I watched her weave lies. Our life was breaking apart, it had been broken already, all we were doing now was riding it out, until she left . . . . Wilkinson was no more than a small grotesquery.

We ate dinner in almost complete silence. I continued the argument privately. She went in to take a bath. I picked up a book, tried to read, but couldn't. I walked into the bathroom.

"I'm sorry," I said.

"It's all right," she said. Her hair was wet. As she lay back in the tub her body seemed to shine in the water. In spite of everything that had happened her body retained a softness and innocence. I felt it pulling me back.

"It was a stupid thing to fight about. Really. Makes me feel . . . abashed."

"Abashed?"

"Ya." We both laughed.

"Come here," she said. I went over and sat on the edge of the tub. I leaned over the water and kissed her.

"You taste like shampoo," I said.

"Are you all right now?"

"Yes." I felt a mild irritation at her question, as if our fight had been caused merely by an irrational tantrum.

"What happened this afternoon wasn't anything. Really."

"If it wasn't . . . ." I stopped.

"What?"

"Nothing."

"Say it."

"If it wasn't anything, then why do it?"

"Why? Because it was flattering, maybe even mildly instructional, and it didn't hurt anybody. Chalk it up to experience . . . ."

"Experience is bullshit!" I felt the anger return, like a slack rope being yanked tight.

"Stop it."

"I won't stop it. All that fancy talking we did about the theory and practice of freedom, about being open to change . . . I didn't realize we were including cheap propositions . . . ."

"Maybe it does include that."

"It really disgusts me."

"That's because you're a Puritan."

"And you? What are you? Going around putting notches in your belt."

"I'm leaving in a month. If that's not soon enough, you can leave."

"Okay, I will." I listened to my words as if they had been spoken by a stranger. I turned and walked out. She lay trapped in the bathtub. I went to the closet and took a coat out, sending the hanger clattering to the floor. I heard her call to me. I didn't answer. I opened the door and waited. Perhaps for her to say some magical healing word that would dissuade me. Too much had been said already.

Gene angry at D. now—doesn't want to see him again. Gene found out that D. told Abigail about me—in general, rather casual terms as a married woman he has whenever he wants. This got passed on to Hugh and Michelle. I believe he might have said it. It does not bother me terribly except

*that it is a dishonest image, part of D.'s immaturity and
need to confirm his masculinity. For G., however, it's
humiliating, and I understand his anger.*

I let the door slam shut. I ran down the stairs and out
into the dull, cold night.

That night passed like a dream, like a fierce, stubborn
performance. I was weak and tired before I began, but I
took the subway downtown, let the crowds carry me as if
I was weightless, carried on by sailors and gangs of black
teenagers, frightened old men who clutched their newspapers and worried their way molelike down the street. A
tough young girl jabbed flowers at my chest, shouted at me
to buy. I walked up and down in front of movie houses, a
dozen times fighting down the temptation to call her.

Instead of calling I bought a ticket to *Point Blank* star-
ring Lee Marvin. I sat motionless through two hours of an
ex-con carrying out elaborate revenge, kneeing, hitting,
shooting. When it was over I got up to get a Coke. The
lobby seemed to have been lit with dust. The phone was
out of order. I stared at the clock, thought of her, imagined
her calling our friends. I went back and sat down.

The second feature was a very bad Tarzan film, a long
way down from Johnny Weissmuller. I sat through it. It
occurred to me what a stupid and immature thing I was
doing. I sat through *Point Blank* a second time, watching as
the theater emptied around me. My body began to ache
with fatigue. The light on the screen seemed to grow more
intense, glaring over every grain and pore on Marvin's face,
the voices began to grate and distort. Lee Marvin was playing it tough all the way. A drunk a few seats in front of me
babbled back at the screen, filled with some private, incomprehensible rage. He went on intermittently for half
an hour and then fell asleep. I got up and left.

I took the subway uptown and stood across the street from our apartment. I watched the dark windows catch the sudden flash of light from cars passing in the street, and just as quickly wanted to be back with her. I thought of her asleep and alone, yet it was impossible to go back now.

It began to drizzle. The particles of water danced around the streetlights like a swarm of moths in summer. Down the street I could see the Greeks at the fruit stand rushing to cover the vegetables. They laid out huge sheets of plastic, working in a pool of light. I stood watching them for close to half an hour. A policeman came by once, twice, the second time stopping to ask me if anything was wrong. I said no and walked on.

I met a Puerto Rican streetwalker on 96th Street, next to the Ping-Pong Parlor. There was no one else in sight.

"How are you?" she said. She was small, chunky, with a round face that made her look like a Spanish Little Orphan Annie. I could have sworn she had a tooth missing. This was not a high-priced whore.

"Not so good."

"No?"

"No."

"What you need is a little company."

I didn't even have the heart to ask her how much it would cost. "I don't think so."

"It would cheer you up."

"Does it cheer you up?"

She shrugged and grinned. "Sure, why not?"

"I don't think so. I just had this fight with someone. Someone I love very much."

"Your wife?"

"Yes." She looked very somber. "What are you looking so sad about?"

"Nothing . . . ."

"It has nothing to do with you. You must hear stories like this fifty times a day."

"No."

"Ten, then."

"What are you getting mad at me for?"

"I'm not mad at you." It was raining harder. "This is stupid. We're both getting wet. It's not worth it. You'll catch a cold and then where will you be?" I turned and walked off.

"A little company . . . ." she said. "You'll feel better."

There is all this wildness in me now that has to be played out, even when it is dangerous and self-destructive. And there is Daniel, staring through me, penetrating and struggling with himself, can't understand why he relates to me at all any more, yet can't quite say, "No, we are not going to see each other again." So I try to be detached and I can do it if he is, but knowing if he said, "Let's try to make it work—come with me—be mine for a while," I would have great difficulty saying no and maybe I couldn't. Yet we continue to have it out—the hostility he feels, the harshness and the analysis of each other and now I am feeling of less worth to him, but he challenges me to face it all and be honest with myself and he pushes me to use my power and yet I cannot quite win from him. So we fought, played a "skirt the issue" game, then poured out truths after we had slept together again—this time for me so I could say he didn't decide the "never again" and so I could say, "See, I can sleep with you, enjoy sex—yes, I do enjoy sex with you, but take it for that and I am not emotionally involved." Did I win or lose? I don't know.

I got back on the subway. The floor of the car was spattered with soggy newspaper. I rode for more than an hour, half-asleep, all the way to the end of the line, Coney Island.

The pizza stands and game booths of the summer were all boarded up. The huge black skeleton of the roller coaster stood against the gray morning sky like the subdued remains of an ancient beast. I walked along the boardwalk, then down across the raked sand. The seagulls pecking for food scarcely bothered to strut out of my way.

I looked out over the water. When I saw the man he seemed no more than a small dark stone balanced among the rocks jutting out near the end of the pier. Then I was able to see his fishing rods fanning out like antennas. He wore a heavy rubber raincoat and hat, turtlelike, and he didn't seem aware of me at all. I felt a sudden impulse to run to him, to tell him, but no, there were no further gestures to be made, not to strangers. There was nothing to do but go back. I watched him for a minute longer.

I rode the subways with the morning rush, crushed between bright-faced Catholic schoolgirls in blue jumpers and businessmen wedged in behind their morning *Times*. I clung to the iron strap, trying to stay awake. As I nodded and jerked back and forth between waking and dreaming there was a moment when I thought I saw her moving through the car just ahead of me. I suddenly became aware of people staring at me. I caught a reflection of myself in the opposite dark window, and realized how exhausted and dirty I was. They had a right to be frightened.

It was ten by the time I got home. She should have left for work. I opened the door and saw no one; but then there was a cry, neither of joy nor of fright, but her cry, and she started to run to me. Her face was swollen and tired. There would be no showdown. I went to her and held her, rubbing her face with the back of my hands.

Over and over she said, "Are you all right, are you all right." I nodded. "I was so afraid. I didn't know who to

call. I couldn't think . . . I'm so sorry. Look what I did."
She picked up something from her purse. "I was so afraid
that you would come back and just leave for good that I
took the checkbook so you couldn't . . . not without my
seeing you." She started to cry. "I'm so sorry."
"It's all right," I said.
"I need you. I really need you, Gene. I can't do this without you. We'll work something out. We will. We have to."

He said, "I've been thinking about it for the last twenty
minutes—can I come to live at your house for a week or so
before I go?" Shock and yet yes, oh, yes—but I know that
what may be your inclination today may not be tomorrow.

I remembered the seaman's chest in the middle of the
living room. It was late in the afternoon. I could call REA
the next day. Another day wouldn't matter.

I took the subway uptown. The January afternoon had
turned bitter, the streets were freezing back into ice. I
stopped in the market to pick up some food and wandered
into the Mill Luncheonette to thumb through magazines.
There was no rush. The cashier glared at me. I put the
magazine back in the rack and smiled.

I opened the door; everything was as still as a photograph. Every detail was the same, the books, the magazines
jammed in the wicker basket, the chair askew at the desk,
the trunk sitting in the center of the living room. The only
fact that was changed was that she was gone. I threw down
my coat, turned on the radio, went in and lay down on the
bed.

I stared out at the high buildings across the street, at
the gleaming water tower, at pigeons perched in dark windows. I turned, held a pillow as if it were a body.

In the stillness the thoughts came fast, tumbling on top

of one another. If I had been different I could have changed it. If I had been stronger, angrier, less jealous, more patient, if I hadn't been so weak I could have made it work. It was so agonizingly clear. How the finest impulses we had had turned on themselves, how freedom had enslaved us, how love took on the face of weakness. None of it had to happen the way it did. It would have been so much easier to bear if I could have believed it was inevitable. It wasn't. It was only mistaken.

It happened suddenly, as if I was being shaken by a small, desperate animal. Hold it, hold it, be a man, shake it off, walk it off . . . I didn't have the strength to hold it. I started to sob, deep, loud sobs that sounded strange and alien, crying because things had ended, I had loved her, she loved me, no matter what had happened, it didn't have to end. I cried because it was merely wasted.

When it was over I lay motionless by the edge of sleep for a long time. I got up, remembering it was time to eat. I went to the refrigerator, dug salami out of the wrapper with a fork. I flipped the TV on and off. I didn't turn on the lights, but let the rooms darken slowly, fading as I lay in the bedroom not sure how to go to sleep alone.

Two

After Ann left there was a time when the central fact of my life was her absence. It was as if living with her had somehow concealed her from me; hidden her in a thousand repetitive acts of eating, seeing friends, catching a movie now and then, cleaning, sleeping, waking, going off to separate tasks. Now her absence gave her the sudden focus and pain of a splinter pulled swiftly from a wounded hand.

The declared point of our separation was to allow some time to decide whether we would split permanently or come back together in some new way. Inevitably I felt it was more for her to decide than me; though there were times I imagined revenging myself on her by sleeping with a hundred different women, mostly I just wanted her back on almost any terms. I was aware that that attitude lacked a certain amount of pride and I was aware that things couldn't be on the same terms as before. There needed to be changes, big ones, and if I was at times desperate it was because I couldn't imagine how to achieve those changes being three thousand miles from her.

One morning in early March I was wakened by the ringing of the telephone. It took me a minute to get there: I was groggy and a little hung-over from the night before. It was my mother, calling from a Fargo hospital. My aunt Harriet had died. "Oh," I said. "Oh, I'm sorry." I tried to unscramble my aching head. I couldn't think of anything to say. I felt dirty and stupid.

Very quietly, very gently, my mother began to talk. Harriet had been alert to the end and hadn't been in severe pain. She had asked about us and what we were doing. My mother was at her bed the whole day and then in the early evening Harriet had asked if it was still snowing outside the window. My mother got up to look and when she turned back, Harriet was dead.

I stumbled for things to say. My mother asked how Ann was. I said that she was fine. My parents knew that she was in California: I had given them some transparent excuse that couldn't have stood two or three pointed questions. Even now, in this moment of shared sorrow, when almost anything could have been said without fear of rejection, I still refused to say more. I lied; Ann was doing fine, I would be seeing her soon. After we said good-by I went out and walked for an hour. When I returned to the apartment I slept till the middle of the afternoon.

Only later in the evening and in the following days did Harriet's death begin to hit me. The grief came in sudden, numbing waves, and with it, a flood of memories: the summers at the farm, roaming through the woods, playing in the sawdust of the icehouse on hot afternoons, driving the animals into the barn in the early evening and the sense of what then seemed like a boundless affection that Harriet had for us. I thought, too, of the effect that Harriet's death would have on Arnold, living alone now on that farm. Trying to compare the sense of abandonment I felt from separating from Ann and what Arnold must have been feeling then, I was confronted with one basic difference; for him it was final and irreversible.

My mother handled it much better than I did. She had a sense of religious consolation that was no longer available to me. If I had spent years mocking the simplicity of her beliefs, now I envied her their strength. For her, forgiveness, rebirth, salvation, were all facts, no less than the wind rising on the prairie in the afternoon or a wet finger clinging to iron in the bitter cold. They were as much a part of the working out of things as death. For me, the loss of Ann and now the loss of Harriet seemed irreparable.

I remember being baptised when I was thirteen, walking awkwardly down into the water in a billowing white robe, sloshing my way across to the preacher's outstretched hands. I answered his questions in a daze, waiting. I watched him raise the white cloth and cover my face. He pushed me back into the water, his other hand at the small of my back. I fought him for a second, grabbing his hand, and then I felt the coldness of the water closing around me and the white robe billowing up like a floundering parachute. I heard the muffled words above the water and then he began to lift me. I struggled to regain my balance, trying to wipe the water from my eyes, and stood finally, coughing, and stared out at the congregation, waiting for some sign that they believed, or that would show me I believed, that I was a new, born-again person.

There was no sign then and there was no sign now. If Ann and I were to wash away the pain and betrayals we had to find our own way. The other forms were not available to us. If we were to forgive one another, trust one another, we would have to pull it out of our own guts; I wondered if that was enough.

Summer nights on the farm, Harriet would come up to our rooms at bedtime and talk to us or read by the light of the kerosene lamp. It was the most prized part of the day. Gradually, we would drift toward sleep in the half-lit room. When we were asleep she would quietly extinguish the lamp. Only then, if we awoke for a moment and saw the wisps of smoke from the charred wick, would there be a pang, a painful, confused yearning, for that grace that had just a second ago been present with us.

Ann wrote beautiful letters. They were a kind of reminder of the wit and ease we had once shared; on Valentine's Day she sent me a postcard with a surrealistic photograph of two nude female mannequins stepping into a cab in the midst of a forest; on the back she had drawn, in crayon, a heart with an arrow piercing it. We began to write two or three times a week, as often as we had the summer before we were married. Amidst her cutting free of convention she remained a faithful correspondent. It was startling how easily we fell back into the old expressions of affection. Our letters were tender enough to have been written by twenty-year-olds, yet we were careful to make no promises or to plan when we would see one another.

We had one friend who took our separation particularly hard. Michelle and Ann had always been in some ways as close as sisters. Ann's confession that she was having an affair was like dropping a lighted match in dry woods.

Michelle and Hugh, Ann and me: there had been times when it seemed as if our lives were made of interchangeable parts. We had been to one another's weddings, shared politics, movies, friends, come to New York together, and gotten involved in social work and teaching. But of the four of us it had always been Michelle who fought against things settling down, against the weights of complacency. Around her I always felt in the presence of crisis, big emotions, radical responses; she was willing not to be discrete. The irony was that she was the one to have a child, to be forced into a domestic role. It created a lot of tension; she had too much psychic energy to mellow her way into motherhood.

When Ann told her about Daniel, there was a rush of feeling for Ann, of sympathy and identification. It was followed by a pulling back and then by an intense anger.

Michelle said she could understand why Ann had become involved with Daniel, but she thought Ann should end it. When Ann wouldn't it made no sense to Michelle. She accused Ann of throwing her marriage away. Things became bitter between the two of them. The inferences thrown back and forth cut deeper: Ann felt that Michelle was jealous of her freedom, was afraid to face the dissatisfactions in her own marriage, had turned moralistic because finally she couldn't compete; to Michelle Ann seemed arrogant and manipulative—she was having an adolescent rebellion ten years late, blind to the pain she was causing.

It became nearly impossible for the four of us to be together. I don't think we saw them at all during the last month.

After Ann left I began to spend a lot of time with Michelle and Hugh again; they would invite me to dinner a couple of nights a week and we would go to films together. One afternoon I met Michelle with the baby in the supermarket and helped her carry the groceries home. Going into the apartment I brushed against the door and a piece of paper dropped out of my pocket. My arms were full of bags; Michelle bent down and picked it up; it was a letter from Ann. She looked at me with a sudden flash of anger and then slipped the letter back in my jacket pocket.

Very quietly she said, "It's just not fair."

"What's not?" I said.

"Her having it both ways. Her having you and you not having her."

"Stop it. That's not fair."

"No? You don't think she's toying with you? She lets you wait while she's out there screwing around . . . . You think it can be any different than here? Or is she still telling you everything? I don't understand. Doesn't it make you angry?"

"Ya, I get angry."

"Then why are you hanging on to her?"

I stood just inside the doorway, holding two bags of groceries, watching Michelle's child chew on the corner of an old *Newsweek*, and growing angry at her.

"Maybe because I'm faithful to her."

She gave a short, startled laugh. "Does that apply?"

I said nothing.

Her voice softened. "You can't just wait for her. You can't let her do that to you, Gene. You've got to have your own life. You've got to. It's so arbitrary . . . who falls in love . . . who gets married. Look at you and me and Hugh and Ann . . . it could have been any number of other ways. It was five years ago and already I can't remember what my reasons were. None of it was necessary . . . ." She looked up at me suddenly. "She was wrong to hurt you like that. And to go on hurting you. Other people may have good reason to think about the same thing . . . but they can't . . . . There are other people it would destroy." She was looking directly at me, her face flushed and alive. The challenge confused me and I looked away. The kid cried; he had just pulled a pile of magazines down on his head. Michelle reached out, her gaze unfaltering, and took the bags from my arms.

I had a need to spend time with people who didn't take sides. Whenever I went down to Philly to see Evan I felt a strong sense of relief. He had been close to both Ann and me for a long time, yet he didn't push for more explanation than I was willing to give. He became the crucial friend.

Evan was learning to live with a woman while I was learning to live without one. The changes in him were perceptible. He stopped being on the run all the time. There was, for the first time, a part of his life that was private, his own. Being around the two of them for a weekend caused my spirits to rise almost unreasonably.

Part of it was the fact that Sarah hadn't known me with Ann; there was no past to dwell on, analyze, commiserate over. When Evan and I made references to that past, she would look away, try to be interested for a time and then fail; it made us stop talking about it. I found that liberating. There's a special charm about having a crush on your buddy's girl. I developed one.

As the spring went on Evan began talking about quitting his job and getting out of Philadelphia. Too many of his friends were in trouble; he was convinced that the city was itself poison. He talked about getting out, going west.

Sarah was involved in organizing high-school students against the War. The Saturday that they were to march on Fort Dix, Evan and I joined them. It ended up being a very sad day. The demonstration was small and confused, with a lot of aimless wandering, shouting at impassive young M.P.s and some arrests. Beyond the knot of milling people was only the desolation of gray barracks and scrub pine. I was ten years older than any of the kids and when they chanted and screamed I felt that I wanted to tell them it wasn't going to work, I had tried it before. I knew I didn't have that right; I felt very old and cynical.

We drove back to Philadelphia that night. On the way Sarah insisted on doing a radical critique of the demonstration. I became irritated; it seemed to me that she was coping with a wasted day by shoving it away, objectifying it. I told her so. That launched us into a fierce argument that continued after we got back to Evan's. We went round and round; she said I didn't have any framework for looking at objective conditions and I said it was only possible to talk about history when you stood a hell of a long way back. Evan got mad at both of us for being intellectuals.

It was two in the morning and we were all too tired to talk, yet we were unwilling to say goodnight. The three of us finally got the pillows and blankets out and made rough beds in the middle of the living room floor. We lay silently in the darkness.

"Hey, Sarah," I said. "I'm sorry. I didn't mean to . . . "

"Don't be sorry," she said. "We're not done yet."

"We should get out of here," Evan said.

"Escapist," Sarah said.

"No, really. We should go out West. The three of us. Gene, what do you think?" I didn't say anything. I could only think of going out West in terms of seeing Ann and I wasn't ready to think about that. "Gene, what do you say?"

"I promised Michelle and Hugh I'd go up to Cape Cod with them in June," I said.

"You can go to Cape Cod any time, man. I'm talking about a real trip. Really doing some things."

"I don't know. We'd have to plan," I said.

"Sure, we'd plan it. But the three of us, hiking through the mountains . . . ."

"Evan, don't push him . . . ." Sarah said.

"Think about it," Evan said. "Think about it seriously."

Evan talked on for a while, free-associating about small western towns, Cripple Creek and Victor, Alamosa and Trinidad, where we could meet friendly people and watch rodeos. I drifted toward sleep, my arms touching theirs, a hand to my cheek, not knowing if it was his or hers, thinking how to objectify my losses and what I would need to do before I could see Ann again.

In the morning there was a neatly typed three-by-five card in my cereal bowl. I picked it up and read: *So our campaign slogan must be: reform of consciousness, not through dogma, but through the analysis of that mystical consciousness which has not yet become clear to itself. It will then turn out that the world has long dreamt of that which it had only to have a clear idea to possess it really. It will turn out that it is not a question of any conceptual rupture between past and future, but rather of the completion of the thoughts of the past. K. Marx.*

I looked up at Sarah who was sipping coffee and pretending to read the morning paper. I smiled. "You win," I said.

I would talk to Ann almost once a week on the phone. I knew that she was seeing other men. I asked and she told me. I said nothing; as long as we were leading separate lives there were not the same rights to be angry or hurt. Had she seen Daniel? Yes, she had gone to San Francisco for a social work convention and spent the whole weekend with him. They had had a good time, but he was involved with other new girls, it was nothing more than a friendship now. I wanted to tell her she was a liar; I said nothing.

Are you seeing one person more than any other? Yes. At first she didn't tell me his name, as if naming him was a magical act that would make him vulnerable. Larry, she finally said. Larry. He was the same age as Daniel, but seemed older and tougher. He had been in and out of a dozen schools. He had lived on a kibbutz in Israel, been through the drug scene in New York and was now making another stab at UCLA. How close was she to him? Some things she didn't answer.

There were so many things she didn't tell me, that she forced me to imagine out of dropped hints, omissions and indirect references. I vacillated between dark, convoluted nightmares and sudden flashes of hope. The difficulty was that the only way of expressing love to her was to let her go free—we were beyond the point where argument, anger or judgment made any difference—even if it meant letting her drive herself into some dark, poisoned corner. Yet I could not let her go, there were too many things we had shared, she was too good a person and too much a part of me, no matter what had happened. But without ever really knowing what was happening with her, without seeing her, there were moments when there was no brake on despair or the fantasies of violence against her or those unnamed men.

Ann asked me once if I was seeing anyone. I said I wasn't.

"Why?" she asked.

"I just don't feel like it."

"But aren't things lonely?"

"Ya. But I'm not sure that prowling for women would change that."

"No." She was silent for a moment. "There are times when I miss you very much, you know that," she said.

"That would be simple to solve, wouldn't it?"

"What do you mean?"

"Evan and Sarah and I are going to take a trip West. Probably in June."

"You would come and see me, wouldn't you?"

"If you wanted me to."

"June. It would be nice in June."

Hope is tenacious, clinging even to the tremor in a voice three thousand miles away. Admit it, I was still waiting for her to tell me to come and get her.

The hard times were when I would call and she would say that she couldn't talk because there was someone with her. She would call me back the next day.

One Saturday night I had a party at my house. It was loud and raucous. People were spilling drinks down the hi-fi, a gaunt filmmaker was wobbling around the room balancing a peacock feather on his nose and some stranger called George wandered about singing, "Chain, chain, chain," in everyone's face. Eventually the party started to thin out. When I closed the door on what I thought was the last group of stragglers I turned around and discovered a strange freckle-faced girl with a bushy, red Jewish Afro sitting on the edge of the couch looking alarmingly awake. She matched my incredulity with an unperturbed smile.

I knew faintly who she was. Her name was Ellen. She was a friend of Michelle and Hugh's who had come down from Boston for the weekend. I knew that she had been divorced in the fall, had two kids and a good job in some politician's office. I hadn't noticed her during the party particularly, except that she wouldn't dance. There was no reason for her to be staying.

I landed in a chair. "How are you?" I said.

"I'm fine. I'm having a good time."

"Good to hear it."

"You were having a good time too," she said.

"You were watching?"

"I was talking to Michelle about you," she said. "She was telling me about you and Ann."

I got up and started to collect dirty glasses. "Look at this." I held up a half-filled glass with cigarette butts bobbing in it like dead fish. "Obnoxious."

"Michelle is very much on your side," she said. "She really identifies with you."

"You think so?"

"She feels that you've really been hurt. You don't seem very hurt to me."

"I scab up real quick. What are you talking like this for?"

"Because I think I know what it's like."

"What's it like?"

"I know what it was like with Elliott and me. It was Elliott who had the affair and me who got the sympathy. Everyone said how awful it must be for me. Sympathy is very nice, whether you deserve it or not." She squashed the butt of her cigarette out in the bottom of a glass and lit another one.

"Those are bad for your health," I said. I was tired, I wanted her to go. I wasn't ready to get into a heavy rap about disintegrating marriages, and I didn't want to sleep with her; or with anyone else.

"It wasn't the way people thought. I was the one who wanted the split. I was bored, but I was afraid to do anything. So in my own way I forced him into it. Most of the time I wouldn't admit to myself what I was doing, but I pushed him. I was the one who didn't have time for sex. I may even have suggested it to him . . . . Maybe there was even a certain amount of pleasure in watching it happen . . . some pain, sure, but guilt-free, and the same results . . . ."

"I don't know you," I said. "I don't know why you're saying this. You come in here, do a number on me . . . ."

"I sympathize."

"Thanks a lot."

"I'm much freer now. I'm much happier. I've stopped pretending. No more hurt innocence. I make my own life. See who I want to see. I carry my diaphragm around in my purse. Elliott would come back if I said yes. But I couldn't go back. It's stupid to carry around a bag of fantasies."

"Why are you telling me this?"

"You can't tell everyone. Not everyone's been through it."

"It's not that way with Ann and me."

"No?"

"No. I love her. I don't know what it was like with you and what's-his-name . . . "

"Elliott."

"You and Elliott. I don't care. I want to be married to Ann."

"Suit yourself."

"I am suiting myself."

"Okay. Nobody understands and it's late and you're drunk."

"And I'd rather be by myself."

"Sure. Tough it out. But if you ever come up to Boston, I've got room. Thanks for the party."

After she left I sat for a while, then went to the phone and dialed Ann's number. Before it had a chance to ring I hung up.

There was only a short note accompanying the single reel of tape: "This should explain itself. I usually screw things up when I write. Maybe this will be better. Love, Ann."

I borrowed a tape recorder from Hugh and after ten minutes of instruction took it home and set it up in the living room. I punched the start button and watched the tape slither into motion.

"It's odd to talk to you in this way, Gene. I feel a little awkward and self-conscious talking into a machine, but I've been trying to write a letter for more than a week and it hasn't worked. Maybe this will do it. I want to be your wife. I want to be married to you. More strongly than ever before I feel that is where my place is, where I belong. All the wildness and experimentation that I've gone through is over. There is no point in going on with it, trying to ride experience as if it was some great, unbroken beast . . . I'm exhausted, Gene. Everything seems to be going in circles. I'm tired of stupid, selfish people. I'm tired of being one. I try to imagine you in front of me, talking to me . . . I try to picture you . . . try to hear your voice . . . . What I want now is to build a life with someone. With you. I'm sure of it. There are too many crazy people here, danger-ous people. In the past weeks I've had frightening dreams of your being gone, or finding you dead . . . Gene, listen to me . . . I want you back . . . .

"The thing I regret the most is the pain that I've caused. I told Larry that I wanted to come back to you. He took it very badly. He was hurt and went into a craziness like I've never known. He would call at all hours of the night and come over and bang on the door and scream and cry. It was awful, being afraid to let him in and just listening to him . . . . I hadn't realized how deep his dependency on me had become . . . I thought we had talked enough, made things clear enough. I feel I can't trust what people say any more, that they all lie to themselves . . . . But it's done now. He doesn't come over any more. There is nothing more I want here. I want to come back. I don't know how to make you believe me . . . . I want to come back. If we both want it enough, what happened before won't matter. Please . . ."

The tape spun on and on, filling the empty room with her voice, spinning a web of hopes. There were questions I had to ask her, but there was no way. I felt dizzy; the room seemed to compress around me. I got up and moved across to the window. Her voice seemed to follow me. Did she really believe what was on the tape? Maybe it was only a whim. A test. Maybe she was only trying to talk herself into it, make herself believe it; talk out loud and scare away the shadows outside the door. Listening to her voice in the room where I had heard her so many times before and yet knowing that she was not there created in me a series of disjointed perceptions; it was as if her body had fled, been spirited away in some winter bewitchment; it was like trying to judge a rapidly thrown ball with only a single eye. I jerked open the window. It was May and the curtains billowed into the room. Street sounds rushed in, mixing with her voice. I leaned out, my hands in the soot on the window sill, and stared at the people below. There was an old Japanese man with a cane, making his way very carefully over the curb, and a lovely young woman with a shopping cart and three small children weaving and skipping loose figure-eights around her. A light wind bounced paper crazily down the street. The tape had come to an end; all I could hear was the children laughing below the window. I turned back, facing the empty room. The reel spun on, growing thick and dark. In the not quite complete silence I felt things dead and hidden begin to stir, lifted up by wind, joining the random sounds of the street, the movement of light across the window. The reel gathered patiently, waiting for me. Yes, I believed. I wanted her back.

Every Saturday morning from April to September, barring rain or personal disaster, Hugh and I played softball.

There was a group of six to ten guys, all teachers, grad students, or social workers, who met at 68th Street in the park and took on all comers. We weren't overwhelmingly good, but we thought of ourselves as scrappy.

The Saturday morning after I got the tape from Ann, we got into a game with some Cuban guys who wanted to play for money, a case of beer, anything. They were mostly beer-gutted forty-year-olds, but they had batting gloves, spikes and bright team jerseys and maybe that scared us. We should have bet them; we played them a double-header and won both. It was the first brilliant, warm day of the spring and when, in the second game, I hit a home run over a fourteen-year-old right fielder who skittered like a waterbug under the long ball, I chased Hugh around the bases, whooping and laughing. At noon Michelle came with Aaron in the stroller and they sat under the trees with players and wives and the ice cream vendor.

After the game and after we had finished crowing to one another about our hits and marvelous plays, everyone dispersed. We walked through the park, Hugh racing Aaron up and down slopes. Bicyclists spun by, lean and hunched. I fell into stride with Michelle.

"Why are you so happy?" Michelle said.

"We won, right?" She laughed. "And it's spring, finally."

"You know who called us?" she said. "The people with the house on the Cape. They can rent us the place right after school is out." She must have seen me frown. "You can still come, can't you?"

"I don't know," I said.

"What do you mean?"

"I'm going out to see Ann."

She didn't look at me, but seemed to focus on the players far across the field from us. "When?"

"Two or three weeks. I'm going there just to see . . . ."

There's nothing decided."

We walked on in silence. I was determined not to defend what I was doing. I had somehow hoped that Michelle would approve; it was obvious that there was no way.

"And if it goes well?" she said.

"Then we'll come back together."

"And everyone will live happily . . . ."

"Jesus Christ, Michelle!"

"What do you want me to say?"

"Nothing. Nothing," I said.

"So you won't be able to go to the Cape with us."

"I'm sorry. I would have told you. It just happened. You and Hugh have been really important to me in the last . . . ."

"Important?" She glanced at me, daring me to find another word, a more dangerous word, something that neither of us had allowed the other to say. I looked ahead at her son and husband playing hide-and-go-seek around a tree.

"Yes. Important," I said.

"Why are you going?" she said.

"It's a trial . . . that's all."

"Then let her come here!" Michelle said. "Please, don't lie to me. You can't let her do that to you, Gene. Don't you understand? You have to have something of your own. She'll wipe you out if you let her. It's so stupid!"

"So what do you want me to do?"

"Let her go."

"I can't. I need her."

"Then fuck it. Fuck it all."

She was crying. Ahead of us Hugh stood with Aaron, waiting. I stood, helpless and angry, not sure of what it was I had just betrayed.

The first thing that happened on our trip West was getting caught in Friday night Philly traffic. We were undaunted; we felt free, loose, of legal age, and nothing was going to bring us down. We were starting out; I was completely caught up in the excitement of it and, for the moment, the thought that I would be seeing Ann in a week seemed little more than one of the adventures that the three of us would have.

There had been an accident somewhere ahead and the Schuylkill was backed up for at least a mile; flashing red lights reflected off the long lines of cars. Everyone crawled through the waves of heat, edging for position. Finally we worked our way free, past the smashed cars along the guard rail, past the huddle of state police, and we were on the open road, hooting a bit, singing a bit, and the evening sun in our eyes. The trip had started.

It was dark by the time we hit Harrisburg. We switched positions, Sarah driving and Evan sleeping in the back. On to Pittsburgh and the tunnels in the dark, flying by semis on mountain curves, the wind shaking the car as we passed.

We switched again in Ohio and I drove. The soft green exit signs emerged, glowed, and disappeared like an overly precise dream. I must have driven this road twenty times, all those trips from Madison to New York to see her at the end of summer and at Christmas time. Twenty hours, eighteen if you didn't hit rain or snow.

I was asleep when we went through Chicago. When I woke up the landscape was home; cornfields, rolling hills, scattered resort billboards, pickup trucks bumping along country roads and cattle grazing in the still-wet grass.

It was only another hour to Madison, but it would be too complex, trying to tell my parents what the hell I was doing; it was better to go on.

The car was sputtering and coughing by the time we hit the rolling hills of Iowa. We dragged into Des Moines doing a cool twenty miles an hour. It was Sunday and the town looked shut down. We puttered from gas station to gas station until we found a gangly sixteen-year-old who said he'd take a crack at our car. We stood around anxiously, drinking grape soda, while he replaced the points and talked American Legion baseball. As we pulled out he shouted after us, "Easy on those California girls."

"Har-ity-har-ity, har," muttered Sarah.

We whipped through Iowa in the waning Sunday afternoon, maneuvering by a seemingly endless chain of house trailers, past artificial lakes with speedboats and waterskiers gliding over brilliant blue water, past burly farmers playing softball in a grove of trees.

Night came on quickly and we hit a detour that slowed us to a crawl. For hours we crept along on a two-lane gravel road; dust and the lights of oncoming cars glared in our eyes. We were all tired and there was no reason we could think of why we had to grind it out, but we went on, finding a weary pleasure in the rhythm of it, taking some deranged joy in just covering ground. In the middle of the night, somewhere just over the South Dakota line, we pulled over to the side of the road and slept.

The next day we drove on into South Dakota, through the wheatlands and further, into cattle country where things got drier and even more treeless. No one was in the mood to push too hard. We wound through the eerie shapes of the Badlands and up into the Black Hills, where we found a campsite along a lake.

The first thing we did was take a two-hour nap that revived us all. The hardship of the day before was forgotten. The kidding and joking were back and it seemed to me, watching Evan and Sarah tussling in mock-combat, the two of them were probably horny. After dinner I stretched out on the ground and watched Evan zip up their double sleeping bag.

"What are you looking at?" he said.

"Nothing," I said.

"It's big enough for three," he said.

"Being buddies only goes so far," I said.

It was time for me to leave; I knew when I was the odd man out. I said I was going to the car to look for something; I followed a patch up around the lake, I sat in the crook of a tree and watched the sun set and a full moon begin its rise over the water. An hour passed. I heard footsteps coming up the trail.

"Hey."

"Hey." It was Evan. "So we're here. We're out West," he said.

"That's right," I said. He sat down on the ground beside me. It was too dark to see his face. There was the smell of pine.

"Something botherin' you?"

"No," I said.

"Well, something's bothering me."

"What's that?" I said.

"Your pulling away from us."

"Ya? maybe I am. Maybe I'm getting ready."

"For what?"

"For seeing her," I said.

"How can you get ready? Whatever happens happens."

"Come on, Evan, don't give me that crap . . . ."

"I'm serious. Whatever happened before is over. You left it behind. That's the whole point. It's not going to be the same with her, it can't be."

"No, it can't."

"We care about you, you know that," he said.

"Ya, I do."

"Well, then . . . we've got three, four days . . . we should get into it . . . . The Wild West . . . . Shit." He picked up a rock and heaved it far out onto the lake. We watched it splash, shattering the reflection of the moon. Slowly the slivers of light began to move together again, broken rings silently joining with one another, till a trembling form appeared again, riding on the dark surface and what seemed to be an ever-brightening moon lay on the softly breathing water.

We spent the next three days driving down through the Rocky Mountains and it was the way Evan said it was going to be; we got very much into it, hairpin turns, lookouts, streams spilling across the road, high, snowy passes and the long view.

We made the Grand Canyon by nightfall of the third day. The place was packed in tight; the best campsite we could find was a dirt slope the size of a horseshoe pit next to the road.

It looked like the most massive Fourth of July picnic in the world. Besides the endless dust raised by all the cars, there were small fires glowing everywhere in the dark like sparklers, and one luminous Frisbee that whizzed eerily through the trees. We were hemmed in by giant campers, resting in the dark like gleaming farm animals. Lights bobbed through the campground. Four elderly women sat inside a netted, lighted porch playing bridge.

Sleeping was difficult. The sharp lights from the road kept shining in my face, waking me. I would lie there, staring at the figures of Evan and Sarah, asleep together, and think of the days ahead. Once I thought I heard coyotes howling against the canyon wall.

In the morning we ate quickly and went for a look. The parking lot along the canyon edge was a zoo; a carnival of souvenir shops, crowds, honking cars, spilt soda frying on hot cement, rubes in bright Hawaiian shirts and orange socks, loud college kids in convertibles with New York plates and Ithaca College decals, foreigners weighed down by pounds of cameras. Finally the circus didn't matter; when I made my way to the edge and looked down at the glint of the river far below, I felt as if I could look to the bottom of the sea.

The three of us found the path down and quickly left the crowds behind. The canyon walls rose slowly above us and ground squirrels skittered over the rocks ahead of us, oblivious of the thousand-foot drop as they darted in and out.

We must have walked an hour, the switchbacks turning

and turning us in the towers of rock. Heat shimmered on a meadow far below us. The back of my neck and my arms were starting to burn. We sat down on a rock to rest.

"Evan, it's gonna be twice as hard goin' back up."

"Shh!" he said.

"Hey, Evan, how about it?"

"Shh!" We said nothing. It was incredibly silent; we could hear only the scolding of a squirrel, the rustling of the leaves of a gnarled, persisting tree, and the bouncing of a pebble inadvertently kicked over the side. Evan was beaming; we both grinned at him; he had what he'd come for; we were away . . . at least a good distance.

The walk back up was long and it hurt. We hobbled through the parking lot to our car.

"Goddamn!" Sarah and I looked back, wearily, at Evan who stood behind the car staring at one of the rear wheels. There was a dark splotch of oil on the rim.

"What is it?" I said.

"A leak. A break. Something."

We got down on all fours to take a look. Something had sprung inside the axle. It smelled like transmission fluid.

"What do you say we shove the thing down the canyon?"

"Now, Evan . . . ."

"There must be something we can do."

"Yeah, get the thing fixed."

The nearest dealer was Flagstaff. We tried to make a call, but there was no answer. The best we could would be to wait till morning, drive to Flagstaff and hope they could fix it quickly. I slammed the receiver down on the pay phone. We leaned against the glass booth, regarding one another with dejection.

"It's no good," I said.

"What do you mean?" Evan said.

"Going to Flagstaff will take us at least an extra two days . . . it's too much."

"What the hell we going to do?" he said.

"I can't wait that long."

"If the guy tells us to wait, we wait," Evan said.

"I've waited too fucking long already, don't you understand? I've got to get out there. If I have to I'll hitch," I said.

"Don't be crazy," Evan said. "Just take it easy."

"I'm serious. I'm tired of waiting on people, Evan."

"Yeah? Well, this time you're waiting on a broken car."

"Come on, you two," Sarah said. "Fighting isn't going to help anything."

We drove back to the campsite to eat and then headed back to the canyon to watch the sunset, driving through the low pine forest, the road turning black as typewriter ribbon before us.

There were between ten and fifteen people at the lookout. A kid with shoulder-length hair and bare feet squatted yogalike far out on a rock ledge; we found a place along the rail.

Behind us the sun had almost disappeared in the trees, but below in the canyon the walls were still bright, light gleaming off the twisting band of river. The sun played tricks with the worn rock, unfurled eroding shadows miles downward. At the west end of the canyon and far below us, heavy clouds moved in like a shapeless, dark sea animal, blotting out the rocks beneath them. The watchers began to murmur and point as they realized what was happening. The perspective from above was eerie; we looked down on the flashes of lightning, the sudden rain, listened to the rumble of thunder. Birds swirled away from the storm like bits of white paper caught in a draft. Yet around and above the storm the soft light of the sun lapped against spires of rock. The storm broke itself upon the canyon, the clouds dissolved, melting in the wash of light. The storm was gone. There were only fathoms of light, welling up from jagged banks, suffused like a golden powder.

The sun was almost gone. At the rail we couldn't see one another's faces. I felt the tension and the anger of the afternoon wash out of me. People began to walk back to their cars. There was suddenly a clear night sky over us, and stars. The kid in the yoga position had not moved.

Evan and Sarah and I walked back to the car. Evan put his arms around our shoulders.

"Let's go tonight," he said.

"Go where?"

"L.A."

"Tonight?"

"Yeah."

"You think we'd make it?"

"Sure. It's cooler now. That'll slow down the leak. We probably have a better shot at L.A. tonight than Flagstaff tomorrow. We'll get into L.A. early, have somebody look at the car there."

"You're serious?" I said.

"Sure, I'm serious."

"Look," I said. "I'm sorry about before . . . I was being stupid."

"That's no problem now," Evan said.

"What if the thing gives out going down a mountain?"

"Handbrakes."

"Jesus Christ."

"What do you say?"

Sarah and I shrugged. "I say let's do it," Sarah said.

We were out of the campground by ten o'clock, heading west on two-lane blacktop mountain roads. Evan drove first. We were all tired. There was almost no one on the road; our headlights thrust into the darkness like long, shining poles. We drove an hour, then two, twisting through the mountains as the darkness pressed down on us. Finally the lights from a truck loomed up behind us, gaining slowly, overtook us and passed with a shudder, plunging the forest again into darkness.

It was suddenly upon me, like a door flung open. I would see her. The ease and freedom of the trip seemed illusory now. This was no lark, no spree. I was going out to get her, to begin again—anything else was fantasy. As we sped westward, on the desert now and doing a steady seventy-five, I kept seeing her face the way she had looked at me when I had returned after the night in the subways and in movie houses. I remembered how she wanted me then, and yet . . . . My mind went on doing slow-motion coin-flips.

We had to change drivers often. At each stop one of us would take a cloth and check the leak at the rear axle, not that it did any good. I fought to stay awake at the wheel, fiddling with the radio dial; picked up a growly D.J. out of a small Texas station who muttered an obscene patter that lasted a good seventy miles. For a half-hour I chased an old Buick, its red taillights bobbing in and out of view.

I drove on, drifting further and further towards sleep. I began to be afraid, yet I was too groggy to identify the source of my fear, whether it was night driving, the bad wheel spinning out oil, or simply the possibility of seeing her again.

Coming over a hill into Needles I heard Evan shout at me. At first I was annoyed; of course I was awake, I saw the broken white line with perfect clarity; then, growing a degree or two more alert, I realized that I was whizzing down the wrong side of it and that at the side of the road was a twenty-five-m.p.h. sign. I was doing an easy fifty and there was a police car parked at the bottom of the hill.

"Slow down!" Evan shouted.

"I see him, I see him." I eased back into the right lane.

"Then slow down, dammit."

"I am, I am." I started pumping the brakes. "I just don't want to be so obvious, Evan."

I wasn't obvious about it at all. We cruised by the police car doing forty-five. In the rear view mirror I watched the cop pull out to follow us. Evan slumped down in the seat. Holding up an open palm I tried to reassure him; there was a brightly lit filling station a hundred yards ahead. I neatly wheeled the car in and skidded to a stop in front of the gas pumps. The attendant stood up at his desk and stared like a stunned jack rabbit. I got out of the car and leaned on the hood like a savvy traveler, all the time holding my breath as the police car crawled by, looking us over.

Evan lay on his back on the seat. "You're going to get us killed!" he whispered.

"You're exaggerating again. Arrested, maybe." I turned to the attendant who was approaching us warily. "Fill it up, please, regular."

"Were you asleep?" Evan demanded.

"It's hard to say."

"What's hard about it? I'm driving. You can do your sleeping in the back from now on."

Sarah woke. "What's going on?" she asked in a yawn.

"We've just been attacked by Indians. Anyone want any grape soda?" I asked.

Evan drove. I fell asleep quickly, my head bouncing against the cold window, dreaming of things unborn or lost.

When I woke up we were in California. At our backs the sun rose on the desert, beginning to heat up the car.

My stomach was raw and queasy, making it impossible

to go back to sleep. The car raced on, cactus and sagebrush flipping by like some exhausted Roadrunner cartoon. Gradually the desert gave way to hills and huge signs for Bakersfield. The morning filled up with huge trucks and gas stations. We labored up the grade and then, quickly, descended down into a sea of smog that washed over a giant grid of tract housing and highways.

I had been here before. When I was in my first year of high school our family made an abortive move to California that lasted six weeks. The aviation business was supposedly booming and my father was tired of insurance and long, tough winters; the Coast promised new money, eternal sunshine, and fresh orange juice. Our stay in California was short and hard. We rented a small pink stucco house in the San Fernando Valley and the vaunted California sunshine crept through cracks where the walls putatively met the ceiling. At night the blinking lights of the miniature golf course across the alley flashed through my bedroom window. The fall was incredibly hot and everything seemed burnt and stunted: the fruit trees that jammed every tiny backyard, the fifty-year-old platinum blond who came out every afternoon in her swimming suit to water her yard, the gangs of kids who raced motorbikes up and down the flat, endless avenues. My father could not find the job he wanted; after six weeks we packed up and headed back to Wisconsin.

Now, heading back in to L.A., traffic seemed to congeal in the thick morning smog; we hit mile after mile of lights, bumper to bumper all the way. We edged forward, cars jockeying for position four lanes across. We weren't ready to handle it. My nerves seemed to be pulled wire-tight and my body tingled and flushed with fatigue. Being hemmed in by miles of automobiles inflamed us; we muttered weary curses through closed windows. For a mile or so we rode alongside a cattle truck. The animals were crammed tight and they shoved their noses between the narrow slats, trying to see what was going on. I mugged faces back at them.

The traffic finally broke and we shot forward. The names of the freeways began to flash by and we slid across two lanes just in time to catch a Hollywood exit.

We stopped at a gas station to pick up a street map. We laid it out on the hood, next to Ann's letter, to check the directions she had sent us. We weren't far at all.

It took us five minutes to get to the address. We slid silently through the morning streets, almost too quickly. I watched a man on his way to work fiddle with his keys and then get into his car; we pulled up behind him. We were there.

"Okay," Evan said.

"I'll get my stuff."

"Let me get you the number where we'll be staying," Sarah said. "Call us in a day or two. Whenever you want."

"Okay."

I got out and Evan got out with me. We yanked my suitcase out from under the tarps, sleeping bags and camping gear.

"You know where to get the car fixed? Maybe we could . . . ."

"We'll find it," Evan said. "We've got the list of places."

"Thanks, Evan."

"Call, all right? We'll go out and take a look at the ocean."

I nodded and we embraced. I leaned down into the car and kissed Sarah good-by. It was awkward, turning away from them, but I did, and walked slowly towards the large Spanish stucco house. I stopped for a second and, turning back, I waved good-by as the station wagon rattled down the street, coughing clouds of black smoke and then was gone.

Sun filtered across peaceful lawns. It was still very early. She lived in a garage apartment in the back. I walked down the driveway, past an orange tree that was just beginning to bloom. I looked up at the windows that must have been hers; there was no sign of anyone awake. I waited for a moment beside the tree before going up.

I knocked softly at the door. There was no answer. She was probably asleep; she didn't expect me until later in the day. I knocked again. I thought I heard the shower running. I was tired; my hands were stained with grease from the car. I knocked hard.

"Ann!"

My voice rang too loud and then there was only the sound of running water again. From a small dirty hallway window I stared down on a maze of garages and backyards, fruit trees, clotheslines, basketball hoops, abandoned tricycles and tangled hoses. There was no one there. I was suddenly dizzy, fatigue rushing in like a wave, I thought for a second I was falling, but then there was the sound of water running, the shower . . . . There was someone there. I had come too early. We should have gone to Flagstaff, what difference would it have made? She had thought there was time for one last night with him, with Larry, Larry was his name. They were inside now, not knowing what to do, trapped by me. Maybe he was crawling out the window in parody of some bedroom farce.

"Ann!" I could hear the terror in my voice.

The shower stopped and there were footsteps. "Gene?" It was her voice. The door opened. She stood back, half-hidden by the door, a towel wrapped around her.

"Hi," I said.

Her hair was wet and dripping. She laughed, almost embarrassed, clinging tight to the towel. She was very brown and thinner than I had ever seen her.

I held her, carefully, wrapped her in me, pushing her wet head to my chest. She brought her face up.

"I didn't expect you so soon."

"We had to come. We had car troubles and had to drive . . . ."

"I didn't mean that. I just wanted to get myself ready for you." She laughed again.

"I'll go out for a long walk and come back."

"Oh, no. Don't." She put a hand up to my face. "You look so tired."

"We've been driving since nine last night."

"Do you want anything to eat?"

"No."

I stared at her apartment. Even the familiar objects that

she had brought out with her from New York seemed alien in a new context; a brightly striped bedspread, our beat-up clock radio, some odd ceramic animals that her grandmother had given her. There was a new guitar leaning against the wall and a mobile of cord and stone that swayed softly in the breeze from the window. I stared, hoping that the objects would yield some secret.

"You didn't hear me before?" I said.

"Hear you?"

"I was standing here knocking for maybe ten minutes."

"I was in the shower."

"I thought maybe you . . . ."

"I was in the shower. It's hard to hear anyone." There was a frightened silence, yet there was no way to get those words back.

"I love you," I said.

"I love you," she repeated, plunging the words deeper. We embraced again, I held her back and shoulders in my hands. I felt the warmth of her body and yet there was something unfamiliar about it. I moved away and sat down on the bed. Dark nets seemed to swirl in pools before my eyes.

"Are you okay?"

"I'm just tired. Missed a whole night's sleep. We were down in the Canyon yesterday . . . it was beautiful."

"The Grand Canyon?"

"Ya. The Grand Canyon." I took her hand. "The Grand Canyon."

She put her hands in my hair and brushed locks of it aside. "Your hair is longer." She kissed me quickly. "Why don't you get some sleep?"

"In a while. You're just waking up."

"It doesn't matter. How about a warm shower?"

"Oh ya."

We walked to the bathroom. I fumbled with my clothes; I hadn't counted on being shy in front of her. She sat while I took my shower and we talked about Evan and Sarah and the trip and all the things she would take me to see while we were in California. Water streamed down my body, washing suds downward in a swirl, till even the dark stains of oil were gone. When I finished she got a towel and dried my head.

I lay down on the bed. She sat beside me, leaning back, smiling.

"So you've had a lot of adventures," she said.

"A lot of hiking."

"I love you," she said.

I wanted to talk, but couldn't. I turned to the window. In the yard below was the orange tree. I stared for a moment, reaching in among the sunlit tangle of branches and leaves and new blossoms for the words I wanted and then I was asleep. I could feel the car moving, white stripes slipping beneath us, and I could see the wheel, somehow, a shining disc spinning faster and faster, throwing off oil, a painful, piercing whine going higher and higher, till it seemed to explode into fragments of bright metal shrapnel; then, very slowly, it began to reform into another image, of the slivers of light rocking on the water, gently clustering, gathering until they formed a reflection of a full moon on a peaceful lake.

When I woke there was still sunshine, light across our bodies. She was sitting beside me. I had no idea how long I had slept or if she had been there next to me the whole time.

"Hi."

"What time is it?"

"Noon."

I kissed her softly around the face and then pulled her down next to me.

"You know what?" I said.

"What?"

"Your skin still tastes the same."

"Like peanut butter."

We smiled at one another, almost laughing. She reached up and stroked the lines out of my face, touching me gravely, soft as if she was caressing a burn. Everything was still except for the rustle of the sheets. I caught her shoulders and head in my arms and lifted them, we struggled against one another and she pushed away from me. Her hand clutched at the white pillow case and as I reached to capture the brown hand, to free it from its hold, she was too swift for me. I held myself above her on my elbows, not wanting to hurt her with my weight, and then it seemed as if a fine net cast over us and pulled us together, dragging us through a swift, deep stream, twisting and racing, and I lost myself in her.

We lay together for a long time without speaking.

"Hi," I said.

"Hi."

"If we were eighteen and allowed adolescent questions . . . ."

"Yes?"

"I'd ask you if it was good."

"Only adolescents know how to answer questions like that." Then she said: "We have a lot of time. And we love each other. We won't worry about the rest now."

"Oh, Susanna, don't you cry for me . . . ." I sang.

"I'll get you lunch," she said.

I lay naked on the bed, staring out the window. A hunched old woman in a wide straw hat jerked a lawn-

mower crab-wise around the orange tree. She stopped, took
off her hat, and wiped her face with a bandana. She looked
up at our window. There was only a screen between us, we
were staring right at one another, yet there was no sign of
her seeing me.

"Who's that?"

"The landlady."

"Nice?"

"She's all right. She doesn't bother anyone much."

"Does she know that you're married?"

"No."

"So what does she think about me?"

"I haven't said anything to her." I looked at Ann and she
shrugged. "Who knows what old ladies think any more?"

In the afternoon we went out. We wandered through the
Free Press Book Store, thumbing through occult books,
showing each other the pictures. Later, we took the car to
the beach. She drove well. We whipped from freeway to
freeway, whirling past palm trees, movie star mansions, taco
stands, through canyons, past bleached white beach houses
jammed together like old women elbow to elbow on a
bench. We parked behind an old school bus painted in
bright Disneyland psychedelic colors and then walked
down to the beach.

A wind was coming up and the waves were getting big.
Gulls fought in the wind, tossed about in the air. Swimmers
and surfers began to come in out of the water. Some force
seemed to swell and darken the water and send it smashing
against the rocks.

"Not much like New York."

"No."

"You think you'll be able to handle it?"

"The city? Sure. I'll handle it because I want to handle
it."

"How hard is it to leave?"

"I don't know yet." She shook her head. "It won't be hard. There's nothing to stay for. I've quit my job, got rid of the apartment . . . ."

"What about this guy . . . ."

"Larry," she said. "That's over. You didn't have to ask."

That night we hauled the seaman's chest out into the middle of the floor so that she could do some packing. I lay on the bed, fiddling with the radio and watching her work.

"You're really California," I said. "You do drive like crazy."

"Out here you have no choice."

"Nice car."

"Got a good deal too."

I laughed. "Hey, terrific. Where'd you pick it up?"

"Used car dealer, where else? The guy who sold me the car thought he was an operator. Used car lot Romeo. It was very funny."

"How funny?"

"He asked me out to dinner."

"You accept?"

"Yes." I didn't reply. "It wasn't anything. It was a complete farce, a big game. He brought flowers and wine . . . ."

"Greased his hair back."

"Right. Told me how simpatico he thought we were. Very middle fifties, Everly Brothers type. I suppose I shouldn't tell you this."

"Why?"

"If it's hard for you . . . ."

"Who the hell was he?"

"An ex–high-school teacher who got into selling cars for the money. He was very slick, very good at it."

"Selling cars."

"Really, it was a riot. Tried to quote to me from Yeats. Could you die?"

"Yeats."

"Isn't that too much?"

"You only saw him once?"

"A few times. I'd never met anyone who really tried to work a line before. It was a marvelous game. You can understand that."

"Did you sleep with him?"

"It was only a game, Gene."

"Did you?"

"Yes. Once." I waited for her to go on. "You asked me to tell you. Look, it's over. That part of my life is over."

"What did Larry say?"

"That was before Larry."

"And after me."

"Gene . . . ."

"Let me help you pack, okay? I've got nothing to do."

Later that night we lay in bed, neither of us asleep.

"What was Larry like?"

"I don't know."

"Like Daniel?"

"Not very much. He had been through a lot more than Daniel. The point about Daniel is that he's been through nothing."

"Mmm."

"Larry has no family, no one. He's been on his own for four or five years. It makes him a lot harder."

"How does he stay alive?"

"Works at the UCLA library. Sells drugs on occasion. One thing and another."

"Was it hard to tell him that you were going back?"

"Yes, it was hard. Things had gone too far. He couldn't understand. He didn't want to. It was very hard."

"Ya."

"He'd been on his own for so long it was very easy to want something to hold on to, to grab . . . . My God, he's so young. He wanted me all to himself. He was very jealous. He couldn't understand about you and me at all, how I could be in L.A. and you in New York and yet still be so close . . . . We fought a lot."

"I'm sorry."

"There's nothing to be sorry about. It was at an end. There was very little we had in common . . . ."

"Then why did you see him in the first place?"

"In the first place because he just came over and sat down at the UCLA cafeteria. He was very sad, lonely, very bright. Quirky. He was so hungry for someone. There was something very strong . . . ." Ann sat up in bed and took my hand. "Is it all right that I tell you this?"

"I don't know."

"I'll stop."

"Why?"

"I want you to know. I want you to know me. Maybe I have to tell you. Not just for your sake. For my own."

"So tell me."

"A lot of the whole thing was just a strong physical attraction. It was very different than Daniel. I don't think there was a time that Larry came over that we didn't make love. But at the end he was crazy. I was really afraid of him. I don't think I had ever been physically afraid of anyone before."

"And when you told him I was coming?"

"I told him I wasn't going to see him any more. He kept calling, crying on the phone. One night he finally came over and I wouldn't let him in. He started to scream and kick at the door. When I let him in, he started to hit me . . . it was awful . . . I thought he would kill me, there was nothing

I could do. After that I wouldn't stay here by myself. I had friends stay with me, or I'd sleep somewhere else. It was terrible. He was so lonely and so crazy. It was terrible." There was a long silence, neither of us moving. She said, "What are you thinking?"

"Nothing."

"I shouldn't tell you, I know. It's so stupid."

"Then why do you?"

"I don't know. I trust you. I take chances. Who else is going to understand any of it? Is not telling any easier?"

"No way seems easy."

She moved to me, her face against my shoulder. "I don't want any more of that, Gene. I can't go on living like that. It's too crazy. I want to come live with you. I want to be your wife. I don't want to be crazy any more." I cradled her to me and as I rocked her back and forth I felt her thin body shaking as she began to cry. We were that way for a long time. Just before sleep I felt the urge to be driving again, wheels spinning, careening into darkness, pushing away from the night.

We spent a day at the beach and a day running errands. She was anxious to leave and saw no reason for us to be staying longer; the ideas she had about showing me L.A. were forgotten. There was an urgency, suddenly, to wrap it all up. The next afternoon we stopped at her office so that she could say last good-bys. I stood back behind the glass doors, watching her embrace her friends, and then she waved me over, insisting. I walked through the rows of desks and jangling telephones, and shook hands with strangers who looked as if they had the book on me.

Later that same afternoon we met Evan and Sarah and drove to a beach. Four became more awkward than three; perhaps we were all too wary; perhaps Ann pushed too hard to make things funny and easy. Evan was not in the best mood; they had been staying with a rich relative of Sarah's in an expensive house up one of the canyons, complete with heated pool and cocktails before dinner. It made Evan very hostile. We sat high on the beach and strained to make conversation. Behind us a steady stream of traffic droned by; a helicopter throbbed over the water like an angry wasp. A pair of teeny-boppers lay in the sand, the transistor radio between them blaring out the Beach Boys and, "Do you love me, surfer girl."

"Evan, let's go back in the water," I said.

"No."

"No?"

"Let's get out of here."

"What do you want to do?"

"Anything," he said.

We ate at a small Mexican restaurant and then walked down the Strip in the early evening. It only put Evan in a fouler mood; he took the giant billboards personally, scowling back at the twenty-yard smiles of Tim Buckley and Frank Sinatra that presided over the night. Cars cruised by, people staring from rolled-down windows. On the sidewalk people peered and gaped into clubs and restaurants, leaned against the windows of stores. There was a stream of unceasing, restless activity that flowed up and back and finally went absolutely nowhere.

"Clip joints," Evan said.

"What?" I said.

"Nothing but clip joints."

"I can't believe you said that. I haven't heard that one for ten years."

"There's nothing going on here," he said. "Let's go."

"It doesn't take you long to make up your mind, does it?" Ann said. There was a sharpness in her voice that hushed us.

"That's just his country-boy pose," Sarah said. We

walked on and half a block further on Evan put his arm around Ann and said something that made her laugh. Finally he lifted her up in his arms and ran back to the car with her. Sarah and I walked behind, side by side, not speaking.

Sarah and Evan were heading north the next day. They wanted to camp in the redwoods for a while and then hit San Francisco. Maybe they would call a friend of Ann's when they got there to find out where we were. Things were left indefinite.

No matter how carefully you plan, there are always forgotten, last-minute details and in the morning we hauled the trunk back into the middle of the floor so that we could rearrange some of the packing. While we were working the phone rang and Ann answered it. The strain in her voice was identification enough. I carefully folded her thick, red sweater and tried not to listen.

When she hung up she said, "It was Larry."

"I know."

"He wanted to say good-by."

"So he did."

She waited, then gently lifted the sweater from my hands. "He asked me to meet him for lunch."

"And you said you would."

"I'm sorry."

"I thought you said it was over."

"It is over. That doesn't make it any easier."

"For who?"

"Don't make it harder, Gene. Please."

"What time will you be back?"

"By one-thirty. I promise."

I held back. There was no need for cheap shots.

She left at noon. I went for a short walk and then returned to the empty apartment. I sat on the bed staring at the sturdy black trunk. The walls and floors were stripped bare; even the curtains were gone. Somehow I was waiting for her again; it made me sick. I needed a way to strike back.

I rattled the bureau doors open and shut and after that, the closets, each time finding nothing. I fumbled with the latches on the trunk and began removing the clothes. She had everything neatly in its place—I piled everything on the bed; dresses, scarfs, books, posters, some old school notebooks. I couldn't find the journal anywhere. She had hidden it too well. I threw the clothes angrily across the room.

Whatever the journal had to give I wanted, and I didn't care if she knew. I wanted to know what had happened, everything, how many men, how often, where, what she thought of them, what they looked like, how she could want me back and still go off to lunch with her lover the day before we left. I wanted her words to tell me, to explain it.

At the bottom of the trunk was a manila envelope. I picked it up and opened it, dumping pictures on the bed. Three were of him. All three were shot at the beach. The first was a close-up of him lying on a blanket, propped up by an elbow and squinting up into the sun. In a second he was standing hands on hips, a silly grin on his face and, behind, there were bathers ankle-deep, befuddled by shallow water. The third picture included them both—snapped, no doubt, by some Good Samaritan photographer—he had his arm around her and she was smiling. He was serious, head slightly bowed, his eyes in shadow. He was much taller than she, yet very thin, and in that loose embrace their bodies—both tanned, and young—resembled one another's.

I leaned back on the bed and stared, puzzled, at the pictures. He was almost homely—hairy, knobby knees, a large crooked nose, and the dark, hollowed eyes of a sad child. This was Mr. Potency. In the pictures he was always looking down or to the side like some diffident adolescent. It didn't match what she'd told me. I was indignant; it was as if she'd lied to me.

She had simply made him up, carved out a hip Pinocchio lover, created him as she had created me—to fill a need. It must have been easy to imagine me coming to carry her off as long as I was a continent away.

There had been pictures of us too; albums, scrapbooks, wedding pictures. It was a curious and old-fashioned need of hers to collect and make records of things.

She was trapped between; between trying to be free and wanting to be bound, even to the point of not being able to shed a lover of two months in favor of a husband; hoarding and shedding; between refusing to give up anything and the fear of being held too long by anyone.

Sitting alone on the bed, jamming the pictures back into the envelope, I began to cry, I hadn't cried since she had left, crying for the madness of it, the impossibility . . . all of us, including the stupid, young kid, grasping for the same thing, standing on a shore, reaching out for the same toy boat and, with clumsy, anxious fingers, tipping it, accidentally pushing it, gliding it far out onto the water beyond our recovery.

The clock said one-thirty. She was supposed to be back. I packed things back into the trunk, trying to arrange them as they had been before, but it was impossible, who can remember what book was stacked on what book, what records on what records? In the end I just piled the remainder in and slammed the metal top down and locked it.

I was on my way down the stairs when she came into the driveway. She looked frightened when she saw me.

"I'm sorry," she said. "There was traffic."

"Don't worry about it," I said.

Railway Express never did come and we ended up lugging the trunk down to the loading dock ourselves. After that we went to Sears to pick up a spare for the car. The day was hot and sapping, my eyes tiring in the sun. The afternoon trailed off into details and errands and endless circling on the L.A. freeways.

We drove back along the ocean and after whizzing by oil derricks and beach houses and seafood restaurants we found a clear section of beach. The sun glowed over the water like a red mantle. We parked and walked down to the water.

"I used to have picnics here with my friends," she said. "I wanted to take you . . . ."

"But not this time," I said. "Don't worry. I'll catch it in the Sierra Club books." We walked on. Waves rushed high onto the beach and then retreated, leaving the wet sand shimmering. I said: "You ever think how banal this would be if you tried to paint it?"

"No."

"But it would be, though, wouldn't it?"

"Maybe."

"Maybe because a sunset's got no point of view. You think?"

"It's lovely the way it is, isn't it?"

"Ya, it is."

"I knew some painters out here," she said. "You would have liked them."

"Ya?"

"Did I tell you that I modeled for a drawing class out here?"

"No."

"A friend of Larry's had a drawing class. He asked me if I would."

I nearly said something about how she had modeled for Daniel's camera, but then I remembered that I had read it in the journal.

"Was it easy?"

"Amazingly easy. The people in the class didn't find it at all extraordinary that I was nude."

"And so you agreed with them."

"I suppose I did. When you've led as well-ordered a life as I have . . . sometimes the ways out of it can seem rather silly and clumsy."

"It doesn't matter to me what you did here." It sounded like a lie, even to me.

"I'm not creative like you . . . ."

"Stop it."

"But I need to be around creative people . . . to get me out of my patterns. So that people like Howard . . . ."

"The painter."

"The painter. His wife is a dancer. They lead this completely unconventional life."

"Oh, come off it." I was becoming crabby and irritated. "What the hell are you talking about? Lack of convention? What does that mean? They believe in daycare centers and smoke marijuana?"

"You're being unfair."

"Okay, I'm sorry." We made our way out along the rocks under the pier. "I am sorry," I said. "Tell me about them."

"There's no need."

"Maybe there is."

"I've just met so many people here, Gene, that I wouldn't have met in New York . . . ."

"I'm sure."

"They've built their own house up in one of the canyons. It's beautiful, they've designed the whole thing themselves. It hangs out over the canyon on these giant beams and there's a monster picture window that looks down to the sea . . . you can sit there in the late afternoon and watch the fog roll up . . . when you're inside you feel as if you're floating."

"You were there a lot?"

"We would go out for weekends, Larry and me. I'd never been in anything like it."

"What do you mean?"

"It was wide open. People moving in and out . . . . It was all very free."

"Are you talking about sex?"

"I'm not just talking about sex."

"Then what are you talking about?"

She looked at me, angry suddenly, and it frightened me. "Yes, I'm talking about sex."

I took her arm. "Come on, let's go back to the car."

"Listen to me!" she said, pulling her arm free. "People made love in the open. I had never seen that before. It scared me at first. Really scared me. People watching other people . . . ."

"Ann, come on . . . ."

"Why should it scare me? Scare anyone? There's no reason. At first I wanted to leave. Larry wouldn't let me. Some of the people were tripping, stoned out in the corners. I found a couch and just watched. A man came up to me, he was very nice. Middle-aged, a doctor. He knew that I was freaked-out. We just talked. He asked me what I was afraid of. I tried to tell him. He didn't push, or proselytize. He told me about himself, about his marriage, his children. It was sad, but he wasn't self-pitying about it. A nice man."

"It didn't upset you?"

"It did. But it seemed so unreal. There were so many things racing through my head, there wasn't any time to chase anything down." She didn't talk for a while. We started back. I was stunned, but at the same time I felt that what she was saying was inevitable, as if she was merely repeating something that I had already heard or read.

"So what did you do?" I said.

"Do?"

"Did you . . . oh, shit."

"Larry and I went into their bedroom. With Howard and Susan."

"Who's Susan?"

"Howard's wife. Larry was more nervous than I was, I think. We smoked some dope . . . . Everyone knew, really . . . there was no need to spell it out."

"So who?"

"I don't even remember how it began, but Susan and I were touching one another . . . it seemed so easy, so simple. God, it was funny."

"What's funny?"

"The thing you have as a child about what evil is and what will happen to you. And it doesn't."

"No?"

"I had never touched a woman before. Funny. I could kiss her breasts, stroke her thighs and . . . nothing happened. It was a woman's body, that's all, different than a man's . . . soft . . . . Like my mother's or my sister's . . . ."

"The two men watching you."

"Howard wanted to make love to me then, he thought we were beautiful, the two of us . . . . But Larry became very upset. He couldn't handle it."

"You could have handled it?"

"I think so."

"But you didn't."

"No."

"What did you do?"

"I tried to bring Larry back in."

"How?"

"By making love to him."

"In front of them?" She said nothing. "That's crazy."

"No, it's not. Does it disgust you?"

"If it does?" I cried at her. "What would you do?"

"I had to tell you," she said. "Before we left here, I had to tell you."

"I don't want that. I can't handle that. All right?"

"All right," she said.

"I want you to promise me something."

"What?"

"When we get to San Francisco I don't want you to see Daniel. If you do, I'll leave. It's got to be over."

"I know," she said.

We walked back to the car. The sun had dropped into the sea, but I walked head down, refusing to acknowledge it as a metaphor of loss, metaphor of anything.

It was our last day in Los Angeles. While the car was being checked we took a walk around the UCLA campus. It was a bright, cool day, quiet except for the incessant click of sprinklers, and all the buildings shone like new coins. Clean-limbed, silken-haired Rose Bowl Queens and steroid-bloated, blond football players strode back and forth with the ease of extras during a break on the set. I tried to find an old friend who taught acting in the Theater Department, but the secretary said that he was out of the country for the summer.

From across a concrete plaza a long, lean figure moved slowly towards us, the image wavering in the brilliant light.

"That's him," Ann said.

"Who?"

"Larry."

Only for a second did I think that she could have set it up. He had seen us too, and moved, in a curious, head-down fashion, in our direction. I smiled prematurely, recognizing his face from the picture. He wore faded blue jeans, a white t-shirt, and he was barefoot. He brushed his long, dark hair with a hand. He looked tired and washed-out. The only thing I could think of was that there were kids like that working in libraries all over the country.

"Hi," Ann said.

"Hi."

"This is Gene."

We shook hands. I was startled—his hand was soft and cold. He looked from one of us to the other, waiting for us to speak.

"I've been showing him around," Ann said. "The Grand Campus Tour. It's for the *Esquire* Fall Issue." Thank God for wit.

"Uh-huh," he said.

"How have you been?" she asked.

"Okay." He stopped suddenly, not sure how the question was posed or how he might answer it. He looked quickly at me. "How do you like it here?"

"Well enough. For a few days," I said.

"That's about right. I hope you have a good trip." He looked at her desperately. "You too," he said. "Look, I've got to get to work, I'm late."

"All right," she said. It was impossible with me being there. Nothing was going to happen.

"Bye," he said. He turned to go and then turned back, like a child remembering his manners. "Nice to meet you," he said.

We watched him disappear into one of the huge new

buildings. How odd that seeing him should be such an anti-climax. A day before, or two days before, it might have been different, but too many repetitions had changed it.

I took Ann's hand.

In the morning we headed north through fog and morning traffic. We drove along the ocean for a while, past a string of drab restaurants and bars, and then cut inland, against the flow of commuter traffic, out of the city, past ranches and open fields, north through rolling hills and after an hour the sun cut through the clouds for the first time, dappling the high meadows. We held the car at a steady eighty m.p.h. We didn't talk much, wrapped in our own thoughts.

By noon it was blistering hot. We were in farm country, mile after mile of artichokes and tomatoes and fruit trees and giant billboards announcing winetasting at the local monasteries. We stopped only for gas. The heat was intense enough that we didn't want to move out of the car; instead we handed the credit card through the window, careful not to touch an arm against the burning chrome.

We were exhausted by the time we hit the tangle below Oakland. Somewhere we made a wrong turn and ended up running a thirty-mile gauntlet of stop-lights, road work, oil trucks, and drive-ins. We made our way into Berkeley and, finally, Jessica's house.

Jessica was a childhood friend of Ann's and now a doctoral candidate in English at Berkeley. She was a tall, pale girl who still bent forward a bit as if abashed by her height. She had been a year ahead of Ann in school and she towered over her in a melancholic and almost maternal way.

We exchanged embraces at the door and then Jessica led us into dinner. We ate and Jessica made stabs at conversation. I was too tired to be polite and right after dinner we went to bed, falling asleep without a word.

In the morning we ate breakfast with Jessica in the kitchen, newspapers sprawled across the table. She told us about her last summer in England, playing Frisbee in the lake district with the children of friends and reading Wordsworth in a small country library. I found her charming and kind.

Suddenly, in the midst of all this, Ann stood up and asked if she could use the phone. When she left the room it was as if all the air had been sucked out, leaving only bewilderment. Jessica asked me something about my work. I misunderstood the question and answered badly. I could hear Ann's voice in the other room. Jessica and I talked a bit longer and then she excused herself; she had to go to the library to do some work. I heard her say a word to Ann and then the door slammed shut.

I sat at the kitchen table, brushing toast crumbs off the morning paper. There was a picture of Willie Mays, the aging Say-Hey Kid. I remembered an old *Life* magazine article about him playing stickball on the streets of New York. What was he doing out here?

Ann stood quietly in the kitchen doorway.

"So?" I said.

"So what?"

"Is he here or not?"

"Yes. He's here. He's going back to L.A. tomorrow."

"So that was it."

"I said I would come over."

"You made a promise."

"For just a couple of hours. That's all. You can come with me if you want."

"You can't keep doing this, Ann!"

"I'm sorry. I'll probably never see him again. It's not going to matter . . . ."

"Do you have any idea what you're doing?"

"Where are the keys?"

"Ann!"

"Please, give me the keys." Her voice was calm, but when she held out her hand it was shaking.

"I wish I knew how to hurt you," I said.

"You do fine," she said.

"I don't know where the keys are. Look on the table by the window." She started to go. "What do you expect me to do?" I said.

She looked back and shook her head, her face flushed. It was only a moment and then she left.

It was so clearly impossible now. How stupid it had been to believe her, to believe that things were going to return to normal, to believe her saying that it was almost over and almost over and almost over again . . . . I had been a fool to come all the way across the country to retrieve something that had been irretrievable a long time ago.

I should have left. Not to leave was a concession, much too big a concession. I should have gotten my stuff from the suitcases and taken enough of the travelers' checks to buy a ticket home. No, be a bastard, take them all.

I called United Airlines. There was a two o'clock flight, San Francisco to Kennedy.

"Would you like first class or coach?"

"What?"

"Would you like us to reserve a seat for you?"

"I don't know."

"What?"

"I'm sorry. I . . . I'll call back. My plans aren't certain. All right? Is that all right?"

"Thank you for calling United." Her voice was curt.

I hung up. I had to think. I would have to take a bus in. But she would be back too soon, she would know where I had gone, she would get to the airport in time . . . .

In the time it took to plot, everything had changed. From a hard decision to leave her, to hurt her, I had passed into another scheme to make her want me again. The moment I might have left her had passed; I was tired; I waited for her to come back. There may have been no hope, but I had to talk to her, there had to be explanations. I felt a great sadness for her.

The phone rang. It was Evan.

"How you doing?"

"All right."

"Really?"

"Sure. Where are you?"

"Here."

"Here?"

"Berkeley. Isn't it good to hear from me?"

"It's terrific. I thought you were camping."

"It was great. Campfires, babbling brooks . . . . But we had to come to see you, man . . . . What's the address over there?" I gave it to him. "Are you doing anything?"

"No. Nothing. Why don't you come over?"

"Is it all right?"

"You don't have to be so goddamned concerned, Evan."

"I'm not concerned."

"Okay. Just keep a little room for me in the station wagon, all right?"

"Don't mess around. Whaddya say we drive into San Francisco and have a good time?"

"Come over first. Then we'll decide."

"See you in ten minutes."

Evan didn't arrive in ten minutes, but Ann did. She was quiet and almost sad, but the tension of the early morning was gone; she seemed nearly relaxed. It had been the same after she had seen Larry.

"I thought you'd be gone," she said.

"So did I. Sometimes I surprise myself."

"Daniel said to tell . . . ."

"I don't want to hear about Daniel. Evan and Sarah are coming over."

"Really?"

"Ya. We're driving into San Francisco with them."

"Gene . . ."

"Just forget it. Just forget the whole fucking thing."

We took Evan and Sarah's car into the city. It didn't take them long to figure out that something was very wrong. I felt numb and unable to maintain any pretense. Ann and I had always prided ourselves on our ability to feign composure; this time it wasn't working. It was very bad and very raw.

After an hour of wandering along the waterfront we stopped to eat at a Greek restaurant. Conversation was minimal and Evan was getting angry about it. A small band straggled its way on stage and a couple of waiters tried to coax the women customers out to dance with them as the music began an uneven swell.

Sarah said to me: "I don't see how you can go on like this." I looked quickly at her and then at Ann across the table. The music was loud enough that it didn't matter what we said.

"I know," I said.

"I'm sorry." I couldn't say anything. "If we could help somehow . . . ."

"Don't let it get to you, okay?" I said.

"Why not? It's gotten to you."

"There's no need to drag everyone into this."

"We're already in it."

"Don't let it spoil your vacation."

"You don't need to be ironic with me," she said. I looked

at her, not sure how to take that. "Really, you don't," she said, more softly. "Let's dance, all right?"

I didn't know how to do Greek dances, but it didn't matter. We got up and linked arms with the red-jacketed waiters and the middle-aged women with bouffant hairdos. We mimed it, we faked it, threw in a little Hava Nagilah, clapped our hands and stomped our feet. Sarah knew how to move, she picked it up quickly. She had an easy athletic grace and we started to ride with it; everyone was smiling at one another. The place was small and warm, sweat began to stream down our faces. We stopped only to drink wine. Evan and Ann sat quietly at the table talking. Sarah was very beautiful; it was straight out of a hundred songs from the late fifties, but I was into it; we laughed and clapped and she kept smiling, keeping me in it, not letting me fall outside. A big woman in a glittering silver dress kicked off her shoes, one of them landed on a table next to the feta cheese, and everyone whistled and applauded and she teetered and jigged in the middle of the floor. Then everyone danced together, spinning around the room, I was arm in arm with Sarah. When I looked back at the table I saw Ann watching me, she seemed very sad and serious, and then the sweep of dancers pulled me away again.

We drove back to Berkeley in silence. It was late. When we got in Jessica was in tears; a boyfriend who was supposed to be flying in for the weekend had called and said he wasn't coming. Jessica had a fever; she took an aspirin and went to bed. Evan and Sarah unrolled their sleeping bags on the living room floor and Ann and I went upstairs.

We got into bed without speaking and lay still, frozen. I felt the anger mounting in me, I had to break it. I moved on her. She was frightened at first, she didn't understand, we fought almost, she tried to push me away. I was stronger than she. I had something to prove; I would be rough and hard, I would will it. I pushed her down in the darkness, holding her, then not holding her, shoving her away. We struggled against one another. I pushed quickly into her, trying to fight back the craziness, but instead only sank deeper, sensing strange bodies around us in the dark; some watching, others bending over us, curious, holding us down with their hands, then lying down, twining their arms, their legs with ours. I twisted my body away from her, hiding my face, trying to escape. I felt my body panic, then flee; I came almost at once. I lay down on the bed. She got up and went into the other room. I was shaking.

In the morning Evan and Sarah left. They were going to see a friend of Evan's at Davis and then head north into Oregon. I felt a strong impulse to go with them, but there was no way to do it.

Ann and I wandered through the Berkeley campus. There was going to be a rally that night and pamphlets and bullhorns were everywhere. The day before no one had expected it to be much, but it had received an unexpected boost—the mayor had decreed that first of all they couldn't hold a street rally without a permit and secondly that no permit would be issued. The students answer was that they would meet with or without a permit. The governor was called and the morning headline ran, "Police Say No," instantly giving the rally the status of a free Grateful Dead concert.

In the sunshine of the early afternoon things seemed tranquil enough. High-school teachers in short-sleeved shirts hurried about buying their books for summer school, some children tried to corral a small dog on the steps of Sproul Hall, and just inside the gate a white-robed itinerant prophet was preaching to a potluck and rather inattentive audience.

In the daylight things didn't seem as bad as they had the night before. It had been a freak-out, right, but maybe that had been necessary to clear the air. Berkeley looked a lot like Madison and there were sudden rushes of how free and easy things had seemed then, the long, roundabout walks down to the lake Ann and I had taken on our way to the library. Five years before. I began to relax. We were on our own finally, no longer surrounded by a thicket of people and tasks; Daniel was gone, Evan and Sarah gone, there was no packing to do, nothing, we were free. Maybe it was just the sunlight and the expanse of green lawn, but I felt the inevitable return of optimism.

"You want to sit for a while?" I said.

We found a sloping bank of grass and lay down. It was late afternoon and the sun was directly in our eyes. She sat above me, half turned away.

"How are you?" I said.

"I can't go back with you," she said.

I spun around, not believing that she had said it. "What do you mean?"

"I can't go back with you. I'm sorry. You can hate me if you want . . . I couldn't blame you. But I can't go back now. I'm not ready."

"Why?"

"I don't know why. I thought that everything was so clear. I had it all set in my mind. I don't know what's happening to me . . . ." She started to cry. I pulled myself up beside her and put an arm around her. People walking by looked up at us, saw her crying.

"Is it because of last night?"

"No, not that."

"I was crazy. Out of my head. And stupid. I'm sorry," I said.

"But I make you crazy, don't you see? In your letters,

before you came, you were so much stronger . . . . When we came together I took all that out of you. You started waiting for me again. I hate it, Gene. I knew what seeing Daniel meant. I should be able to control that . . . ."

"What do you want me to do?"

"What do you want to do?"

"I have no idea."

"I wanted to come back and be a wife to you . . . to be strong and help you be strong, but I can't."

"Where will you go?"

"I don't know. Back to L.A. for a while. There is no other place. I can stay with a girlfriend."

"Not Larry?"

"No. I don't want to see him. Not now. I want to figure things out by myself. Does that make sense?"

"It does."

"I know what it means," she said.

"I don't understand."

"I know it could mean that it's all over."

I grabbed her hands. We sat, holding each other awkwardly. For the first time in a long time she sounded as if she wasn't sure; it made me feel very close to her. The infuriating composure was gone. The pain and sense of contradiction she felt stood next to my own.

"Listen to me," I said. "I love you. I'm sorry too. But you go back and do whatever you need to do. Get whatever help you need. If I can help, I will. Take care of yourself. And I'll wait as long as you want me to."

"I don't deserve that."

"It's not a question of deserving anything. Come on. Let's walk." I stood up and reached for her hand. She looked up at me.

"I can't think of us not being together."

"Let's go."

We headed down Telegraph Avenue. The streets were filling up with kids. Freaks raced back and forth, dodging among the cars. All the radical organizations had people handing out literature. We were in no rush; we talked to pamphleteers, looked at books, meandered through the crowds.

"I can take a plane back tomorrow," I said.

"You could stay a couple of days. I'm sure Jessica wouldn't care."

"I'd rather not have to tell her stories."

"Okay come on. I'll buy you a present."

The rest of the afternoon she was kind, attentive, and funny. The pressure was off and we moved through the growing, excited crowds with expressions on our faces that must have seemed close to bemusement. We ate dinner by ourselves. Afterward we took a walk through the streets behind Telegraph. Police cars lined the quiet, shaded streets. In an empty lot buses were unloading cops.

The police stood in small groups, smoking and talking. They wore helmets, leather gloves and high boots. There were jumbled piles of equipment; guns, clubs and gas masks, the masks looking like elephant heads torn from a thousand trophy rooms. The police stared up at us as we passed as if there were some crime involved in merely seeing them prepare.

I wanted to stay; Ann didn't. The idea of confrontation excited me. We walked back to the Avenue where the street was now jammed and most of the stores were boarded up. Kids hung out the windows up and down the block like old folks in New York on a hot summer night. Organizers hassled their way through the crowd, dropping urgent messages on one person, then another. Though we couldn't see him, there apparently was a speaker on the podium down at the corner. We could only make out bits of what he was saying; the amplification was not good. It didn't matter. What mattered was what the cops would do.

Their amplification was great. In a powerful, megaphone voice that brought back echoes of the announcer for the Lone Ranger came, "This is the Chief of Police. I am empowered by the County and the City of Berkeley to ask you to disperse. I am going to ask you to leave quietly. Anyone who does not leave will be arrested."

"Sir, sir . . . ." It was someone from the speaker's platform. "Would you come up here and talk with us . . . ." Then came a babble of voices and I couldn't make out what was being said.

"I'm going to ask you to clear the streets peacefully. If you do not . . . ." Jeering and booing drowned him out. The radicals had the home court advantage.

"Hey, they're at the corner! The pigs are here!" Everyone forgot about the negotiators. A formation of police had marched to the front of one of the side streets.

"Come up and talk with us . . . ."

"Jesus, look at that. Paratroopers!" A cowboy-hatted, blue-jean-jacketed neighbor pointed upwards. Police lined the roof.

"Gene, let's get out of here. People are going to get hurt," Ann said.

"I want to see."

"Please. There's no virtue in staying around to get your head beat in. It's useless. You can read about it in the paper."

"I'm not worried about my virtue."

"I really don't want to stay."

"Let's go then."

We pushed our way out of the crowd and back toward

Jessica's house. Halfway down the block we heard the dull pop of tear gas canisters going off. When kids started to run toward us we ran too.

We sat on the steps of Jessica's house, listening to the shouts. Across the street from us a boy came high-hurdling over a picket fence and then across the street. He ran by us, up the steps, jerked to a stop like a frightened mannequin, checked to see if there was anyone still after him, and then collapsed, out of breath.

"Are you all right?"

He nodded, still not able to speak. "Yeah. Sure." He wiped his eyes and nose. "It's so stupid . . . I mean, man . . . . It was going to be all right, you know? Everyone was going, they were movin' everybody right on down the street, there was nothin' but shouting going on, there wasn't going to be any trouble. I was right in front of it, I saw it. There was no need."

"Then what happened?"

"They were just clearing the street, this big line of cops, and then somebody let loose a tear gas canister right out in front of everybody and it forced all the kids right back up into the lap of these cops and then everything broke loose."

"Are people getting hurt?"

He snorted. "What do you think? Look here. I got separated from my buddy. I gotta go find him. I gotta get a ride home." He took off down the street. We could taste the tear gas in the air now.

"I'm going to go up there," I said. "I'd rather go by myself."

"Go ahead then. Just be careful."

As I walked toward Telegraph Avenue I could see the whirring red lights of police cars flash off the surrounding buildings. The block immediately before me was almost deserted, but farther ahead figures dashed back and forth like the flickerings of a shadow box. Then, close to me, I heard the shattering of glass. Someone sprinted across the street. There was a shout behind him to stop, but he gave a hip fake and disappeared into a doorway.

A police car slid down the street, its lights out. I saw the door open, the canister drop and explode. I whirled, looking for something to throw. It made me angry, the gratuity and waste of it; but it was no different than before, I always felt things when it was too late to do any good. The cop at the wheel saw me. "Hey, you!" He pointed at me and I waited, dumbly, but they didn't stop, just kept cruising on down the street. I stayed, letting the tear gas sting my eyes until the tears came, wanting to feel the wetness, but then my eyes started to hurt too much for any sentiment, no matter how deeply felt, and I covered them and stumbled on down the street like a fool.

Later, beside her in bed, I remembered something.

"You know what?" I said.

"What?"

"Your trunk. It's coming to New York. What am I going to do with it?"

"Send it back."

"Back where?"

"I'll have an address by then," she said.

She took my head and held it to her breast. I lay against her, not moving, beyond the point of outcry or anger. When I reached to touch her she held my face in her hands, looking at me, and we made love silently, free of any need for assurances.

"We'll have a nice day together tomorrow. Okay?"

"It's a deal."

The morning was fine and Jessica was sick as a dog with the flu. We promised we would buy her medicine and we did, after making a stop at a travel agency to buy me a plane ticket back to New York.

At the dime store we found a dollar-ninety-eight doctor's kit and then we wandered from store to store collecting things to fill it: Kleenex, Band-aids, M&Ms, marbles, jelly beans and a rubber mouse. The streets were full of shopkeepers sweeping their sidewalks clean of glass and boarding up broken windows; altogether it presented a picture of rather jovial industry. On our way back we added flowers and ice cream and when we burst into Jessica's bedroom we both imagined ourselves as Santa Claus.

Over all protest we propped her up in bed, ate ice cream, played jacks on the night stand and told stories. We told her that we would be leaving later in the day and when she objected we bullied her out of being hurt. Nothing more was said about it. Ann and I both got into cheering her up and we laughed and mugged and told her the worst jokes we could remember until she was tired and wanted to go back to sleep.

The plane didn't leave until the evening and we had a whole afternoon in front of us. We drove up into the hills behind Berkeley. She walked ahead of me in the tall, dry grass and I followed her with my eyes. She turned back, aware that I was watching her.

"Are you looking at me?"

"Yes."

"All right then."

She took my hand. We walked on through gnarled trees. It was fine, it was relaxed, just as long as I didn't let the past surge back, didn't deceive myself.

"It's been a nice day," she said.

"Yes."

"The best in a long time."

We told Jessica good-by and headed off to San Francisco. Between the city and the airport, traffic slowed to a crawl because of an accident. A cop waved us on through, past the crumpled cars and the silhouetted figures standing by the side of the road. Suddenly there wasn't much time. There was an attack of panic; I didn't want to be stuck here. We wove in and out of the stream of cars, past the lights of the city, past Candlestick, past the dark weight of the ocean.

We pulled up in front of the terminal and I yanked my suitcase out of the back seat. She got out of the car and catching my hand, kissed me hard. She held on.

"Jesus," she said. "I don't know why you're leaving now."

"Stop it."

"I'll write you when I have a place," she said. I pulled away from her. "I love you," she said.

"I love you too."

I ran, the suitcase banging against my legs, down long, brightly lit corridors, sprinting and weaving through startled knots of people. By the time I got to my seat the engines were running. I jerked my seat belt tight and the roar started and we were moving. We got up in a hurry, no nonsense, the sudden altitude causing sudden rushes in my head.

I rested my head against the dark window. I tried to sleep for a while, but couldn't, my mind tracking back over the details of what had happened to us, what else we might have said. How could she have written those letters? I was tired and the resolution of the afternoon was gone. I stared down. Where were we? It was impossible to tell. Desert, the canyons maybe. I could see only darkness, no point of light anywhere beyond the tip of the wing. Evan and Sarah were somewhere down in that darkness. Ann too. I wondered where she was staying, if she was all right. We had been scattered like husks before a fierce prairie wind. Why the hell was I going to New York? I couldn't think of one reason. I began to drift back and forth between dreaming and waking . . . leaning against the small window, into darkness, waving goodby to Harriet and Arnold, leaving Fargo . . . I had memorized the names of the cities. My mother watched us as we slept, we were going to join my father. I had dreamt of Sioux braves all that night. Emil was dead. Why hadn't they told us? Ann would be heading back to L.A. the next day. Too weary to think, I felt the past lie beneath me like a great, dark map. I fell asleep to the drone of the engines and when I awoke we were circling Kennedy Airport.

It was a hot summer morning and breathing was like sucking a warm, wet dishrag. I got a cab right away.

When the driver stopped in front of my apartment I looked up at the windows and realized that I wasn't ready to face it yet.

"Make that Ninety-eighth and West End," I said.

"I thought you said One Hundred and Thirteen and Broadway."

"I did. I changed my mind. Ninety-eighth and West End."

He muttered a few things under his breath, but we drove down the fifteen blocks. I rang the buzzer three times before there was an answer. I remembered; it was seven in the morning. Michelle opened the door in her bathrobe.

"Can I come in?"

She stared at me without answering. I picked up my bags and walked inside. "Where's Ann?" she said.

"I'm by myself." The toys and magazines littered the floor. There was morning sun on the carpet. I heard the child talking quietly to himself in the other room. "Hugh's still asleep?"

"Yes."

"Summer vacation's making him lazy," I said.

"What happened?" she said.

"It's over. That's all. Over."

"I'm sorry," she said.

"You called it."

"I had no right to say what I did," she said. We looked at one another, speechless for a second. "Can I get you anything?"

"Ya. Ya . . . coffee?"

I swept away half a dozen wooden blocks and sat down on the couch. Aaron toddled out of the bedroom to stare solemnly, thumb securely in his mouth and blanket dragging between his legs. I motioned for him to come, but he stood his ground. I felt dazed.

Michelle brought me coffee and as she set down the cup her hand brushed mine, so softly I wasn't sure whether or not it was deliberate. She moved away from me and stood close to the window, staring down on the street. I cupped the coffee in my hands, hoping it could somehow clear my head.

"How was Cape Cod?" I asked.

"We didn't go."

"You didn't go?"

"I was sick." I looked up at her. "I was very depressed for a time. So many things had built up inside . . . it all seemed to come to a head. I don't know what would have happened if Hugh hadn't been as patient as he was. He is very kind. It made me realize the bond there is between us. It brought us much closer."

"I'm glad," I said. She looked back at me. "I'm very glad."

"What will you do?" she said.

"I don't know."

"Did you really end it?"

"Ya."

"Are you sure?"

"No," I said.

Three

Roadweary and sun-blind, I turned off the cement onto the dirt road; the beaten No Trespassing sign was still there, tilted at a cockeyed angle and peppered with bulletholes. I drove the camper bus slowly to avoid potholes. Blackbirds flew up out of the slough as I approached. It had been two years since I'd been west with Evan and Sarah, but it had been fifteen since I'd been back on the farm; the fact that there were still blackbirds in the slough seemed extraordinary.

The yard was empty. With the first step out of the car my leg almost buckled and I caught myself. I walked up to the silent brick house. The screen door was latched. I knocked but there was no answer.

I walked out to the fields. It was the first of August and the wheat was waist-high. I stared out across the fields, but could see no one, hear no tractor. The grain waved like a rustling, golden sea. I snapped off a head of wheat and tested the hard, ripe kernels. There were butterflies dancing in the grain. I felt tired and weak.

I walked back to the yard and lay down under the trees. It felt very safe and familiar there. I stared up into the silver leaves of the Russian olive trees that rustled in the wind. I remembered the wind, how it would come up in the afternoon and blow all the rest of the day, until late at night.

I lay there till I heard the tractor and the barking of a dog. Arnold was coming in from the field and a small black dog raced alongside, biting at the tires. He hadn't seen me; I got up and walked toward the machine shed. He swung down out of the tractor and I waved. Still he gave no sign of having seen me, but began to walk toward me with slow, stiff strides. His cap covered his eyes.

"Hi," I shouted. The dog leapt around me, barking.

"Hey, Blackie, get down, get down." He held the dog back and looked up at me. For a second I was afraid; I felt like an intruder; I shouldn't have come unannounced. "Hello," he said; as always, there was the shyness in his voice. We shook hands. "Your mother said you were out West."

"I was. I'm heading back now. So I thought I'd come by to see you. See how the place was doin'."

He took off his cap and rubbed his head. "Oh, ya," he said, smiling very slowly. His voice still had a trace of Swedish lilt. He also was smaller than I remembered him. He was physically slight, and, in spite of deeply weathered skin, there was something boyish, almost delicate, about him. He had startlingly light blue eyes and, if it hadn't been for the constricting lines about the eyes and mouth, he would have been handsome. I waited desperately for him to say something.

"I walked out to the fields looking for you," I said. "The grain's pretty high. It must be about time to harvest. Look, if you need an extra hand . . . ."

"Oh, it's not so much any more," he said. "This your car?"

"Ya," I said.

"What do they call these?"

"Camper buses. I'll show it to you, it's pretty neat."

"How far did you drive?"

"From British Columbia. In two days."

He nodded. "You must be tired. Come on in. We'll have a cup of coffee."

We had a simple supper and I went up to bed early. The house was three stories with all the bedrooms on the top floor. I walked up through the sitting room, with its nine-teenth-century stuffed furniture, old Victrola, and, on the walls, the stiffly posed wedding pictures of Swedish immigrants, black-suited men and stern women. I walked slowly up the narrow, spiraling staircase and stopped at the top of the stair. The door to Harriet's old room was closed.

I carefully pushed it open; there was enough light from the hall to see clearly inside. The tasseled bedspread was fresh and spotless. The window was ajar and I could feel the movement of the cool night air. Every detail was unchanged since her death: the porcelain horses on the bed-side table, the pictures of her nephews and nieces, us. It was eerie; as if the past I thought I had left behind was still there and waiting.

Three days before I had been in the mountains with Evan. He had left the East for good and was supposed to meet Sarah in Oregon on the first of September. They were going to look for a farm, maybe. It sounded fishy to me, but I didn't say anything.

As for me, I was feeling footloose. I had a job in New York in the fall, but until then there was nothing but free time. I hadn't seen Ann since I left Berkeley two years before; there had been some hard times, with emotional, painful calls and letters, but I thought I was over it. There had been a couple of friends who were suspicious about my motives for heading west. I told them no, I wasn't planning to see her, maybe it would happen if we got to California, but that wasn't the point. I knew that Ann was living with a man, it didn't bother me. I had been involved with a woman that I cared about very much. I had my own life.

So Evan and I had driven up through Montana into Canada, camping and hiking in the Rockies. We tramped down long valleys with waterfalls roaring all around us and up to lakes where the snow came down to the edge of the water. We would come back to camp sun-burnt, elated and too tired to think. Then one night after dinner I told Evan I was going to the john and instead wandered around the camp until I found a pay telephone booth.

"What number are you calling from?"

"I can't tell, operator, it's too dark in here. I'm in the middle of a forest."

There was the click of someone picking up the phone at the other end. "Hello?" It was his voice, soft and slightly Southern.

The operator said, "A long distance call from Mr. Gene Bergman, will you accept the charge?"

"Just a second, operator," he said.

"Hey," I said.

"Where are you?"

"In Banff. In a phone booth in a campground and I can't see a thing. How are you?"

"I'm fine. I tried to write you but I didn't know where . . . ."

"There really isn't any place. Not till fall. We saw a moose, you know that? Goddamn moose, walking through the campground."

"How far west are you going?"

"We don't know yet." There was a pause. "I'm with Evan. I hope you don't mind my calling collect. There's no way to gather enough quarters out here."

"It's all right," she said.

I thought of telling her about my dream, how I had dreamt a couple of nights before of seeing her, of embracing her, of her being happy to see me. It had been a dream of lightness and ease, but strong enough in its impression to make me want to call her when I awoke.

"We talked about coming out to the Coast. I've got some time, you know. Evan too. We could come down there." She didn't answer at first; I hated the desperation that had crept into my voice.

"Of course you can come. But I have to tell you, Gene, we're getting married. Ken and I. In the fall." She left me room to say something; I said nothing. "It's something that he wants very much. And he's a very kind, very good person. Very much like you."

"And do you want to get married?"

"Yes. It's the right thing to do."

"What do you mean? Right thing to do? What are you talking like that for?"

"Please, Gene . . . . It's not been very easy. He's been very good to me. He helped me out of all that craziness. We've talked about getting married for a long time, Gene, you can't be surprised. At first I would only cry and have these thoughts . . . . Ken didn't understand . . . . I thought about you a lot. I did."

"Okay. Hey. It's going to be all right. Really. Really."

"If you come out here, come see us. Ken wants to meet you."

"That's funny."

"Seriously."

"Maybe we'll come."

"What are you thinking?" she said.

"Nothing. I'm not thinking anything."

"What are you going to do?"

"Well, tomorrow we'll probably go to the dump and watch the grizzly bears."

"Let me know where you are."

"I will. This call's getting expensive. I hope things work out for you. I'm not being ironic."

"You take care."

"Bye."

The phone clicked down. The booth was pitch-black. Outside, fires glowed throughout the campground. I could hear the low voices of parents putting children to sleep inside large, luminous tents. There was the smell of smoke. Up high above the trees I could see the outline of the mountains against the sky; on the highest peaks were still traces of light.

The next day I told Evan I wanted to head back east. He was surprised, a little angry, and wanted to know why. I said I was tired of traveling, there were things I had to do; in fact, I was afraid that if I didn't turn back I would rush out to California to see her.

I drove Evan into Banff so that he could try to pick up a ride west from there. We spoke very little; it was a bad way to end. We stopped in a city parking lot and I helped Evan hoist his pack up on his back.

"You take care now," I said.

"You can change your mind, you know," he said. I caught his glance and looked away.

"No. No, I can't."

As I pulled out of the parking lot I looked back in the rear-view mirror. Evan was standing, rocking from one foot to the other, his giant pack towering over him, as if he couldn't take a step forward or a step back.

I headed east, the mountains shining behind me. I picked up a couple of taciturn hitchhikers east of Calgary. I drove all day across the plains, past Medicine Hat, Moose Jaw, Swift Current. When I dropped off the hitchhikers I didn't pick up others.

She was getting married; I was completely unprepared for the effect that had on me. I had a woman of my own, I had thought that I was free of Ann, that it was far enough in the past. Now I felt as if I had been nursing lies. I held the car at a steady seventy-five, hour after hour. I was incredulous at the idea that I had been hiding from myself some crazy fantasies of seeing her again.

The sun started to drop, glinting off the rippling water in the potholes. It was a long northern summer day and at ten in the evening the sunlight still gleamed across the prairie. Finally the only light was the red lights blinking silently on the tall radio towers. I knew where I was going now. I was going all the way back to the farm—fourteen hundred miles. I was going to see Arnold.

In the morning I woke to the sounds of Arnold fixing breakfast downstairs. The local radio announcer was running down the weather and grain and hog prices.

"You want to do a little work?" Arnold asked.

"Sure, I want to work," I said, grinning.

After we ate we went out and hooked up the swather to

the tractor. It was an anachronistic-looking piece of machinery with a long wooden reel and an elaborate system of belts. I rode alongside out to the field and we went around a couple of times, Arnold showing me how to maneuver the corners, and then he let me take it.

I went on my own, sitting half-turned in the tractor seat so that I could see the reel bend the wheat and the blade cut it, the moving belt shuttling the wheat so that it wove together in a single windrow. I was pretty sloppy at first, turning and cornering, but it got better. The sun began to burn my face and arms. A blue dragonfly hung above the wheel of the tractor; my back ached. The drone of the tractor, the clacking and whishing of the reel and the clapping of the belts became mesmerizing, but slowly I began to cut down the size of the field, the concentric of mown grain increasing around me.

The next day I went out again. Early in the afternoon it started to cool off; it was welcome at first, but then I could see clouds forming. White birds whirled up in front of a black sky. Tumbleweeds started to blow and bounce across the field. Arnold drove out in his truck and told me to head back in, there was going to be a storm; there had been tornado warnings on the radio; he looked worried.

It came with sudden and devastating force. The sky had turned an unreal black and silver and there was a moment of absolute stillness. The wind came, clattering windows and bending trees. Arnold stood silently at the upstairs window watching. The sheets of water pounding the glass made it almost impossible to see except when a sudden flash of lightning would illuminate the yard below, with torn branches rolling erratically like troubled dreamers.

In two hours it was over. We drove in the pickup truck out to the southeast corner. Water glistened in the gulleys and a couple of small sheds had been blown over. We pulled off to the side of the road and walked out into the field. It made me sick; the neat rows of the afternoon were gone, as if they were no more than dust to be blown by the opening of a door. Though there were sections that had been passed over entirely, there were other sections where the wind had swooped down and lifted thirty yards of swathed wheat and strewn it God knows how far. I ran out into the field; there were sections where the wheat had been beaten out like a mat. I walked back toward Arnold. He picked up an armful of wheat and dropped it back into a row.

"What can you do with this?" I asked. He didn't answer. "No combine can pick it up when it's like this, can it?"

"No. Too wide a swath."

"But is there any machine you could use?"

"No."

"Then what will you do, Arnold?"

"We'll save what we can. I'll show you in the morning."

"I mean, Jesus Christ, all that work . . . ."

He smiled at me. "It'll be all right," he said. "It just takes a little work."

In the morning I picked out a pitchfork and filled a jug with water. Arnold gave me a faded engineer's hat that was two sizes too small and made my long hair jut out to the sides like the hair of some mad conductor. We went out to the fields together.

I couldn't believe what we were supposed to do: pitch the scattered grain back into rows that the combine could pick up. We were going to do this with pitchforks. It was mind-boggling; I tried not to think of how many acres there were.

Arnold and I worked from opposite ends of the field. I began vigorously, but was soon reduced to sudden spurts of energy. When I stopped I looked across where Arnold worked steadily with a simple, effortless motion.

"Hey, Arnold, you call this modern farming?" He laughed.

It seemed much hotter than the day before. I threw off my shirt. I began to feel dizzy, pitching in a mechanical daze when a grouse suddenly flew up a row ahead of me. The rows I made were rough thatchwork; when the wheat began to stand up like some unruly cowlick of hair I would flatten it with a smash from the pitchfork. Each time I went up one row and down the other I would stop for a drink of water, resting in a small grove of box elders, among rusted, abandoned farm machinery and the broken kilns of the old brickyard.

I would wash the water slowly around in my mouth and watch Arnold go on working without any sign of letting up. He was so cleanly etched by the summer light, yet shadowed by pain that he and I would probably never speak of.

As the city had moved farther west Arnold's land had become more and more valuable and a stream of real estate agents had come to Arnold to buy him out. He had trouble saying no to people, he was too polite, and they kept after him, hounding him, threatening him with annexation or new tax assessments. One way or another they were going to get him.

As long as his sister was alive he had an ally, but she had died and he was left alone. It was the cruelest of twists; it had been Arnold, a bright, shy boy of eighteen, who had to stay and run the farm when his father was killed. He had never married, living on the farm with his oldest sister while the younger children left, married, had children of their own. Now that everyone was gone they were trying to take away the land too.

His first breakdown had come just before Harriet's death

and the second just six months ago. Depression, they called it, no one could reach him. Both times they had taken him to the hospital and administered shock treatment. Both times it was late February.

I knew about winters in North Dakota, how long and hard they could be. Harriet had told me stories of deer so desperate that they would come up to the house looking for food. With no animals to tend there was no work to be done. The snow storms could cut off the road for days and if you were alone, living in an empty house and men threatening you, telling you they could take that land from you without a struggle, I could understand how it could drive you further and further inside yourself.

It was summer now and there was a harvest to be salvaged. For three days we worked pitching the scattered wheat into rows. I was too tired to think of Ann; there were only sudden flares of emotion like a match that quickly dims. The romance of farm work disappeared as the blisters on my hands grew; I had been stupid not to wear gloves the first day. The muscles in my back and arms grew tight. At times our task seemed impossible; things were going too slowly; I didn't understand why Arnold wasn't panicking.

In the evening of the third day of work we sat out by the pump watching the birds swoop low over the grass in the fading light. The dog chased the birds wildly, helplessly. We talked about farming: the price of wheat, the new machinery, the size of the threshing crews they used to need.

"Who did the hiring?" I asked.

"My father," he said. "He was good at it. He was a good judge of men. They used to have twenty, thirty men here. They used to stay in the bunk houses."

"What was he like?"

"I don't know."

"Don't know?"

"I never really knew him. He worked a lot. And it was a different time then. Children were supposed to be seen and not heard. Then he died . . . ." There was a sadness in his voice. He looked up. "The sky is clear. A good, dry wind. We can start combining tomorrow." He stood up and started walking toward the house; Blackie abandoned the birds and came loping over to Arnold.

The next morning the combine came, followed by a battered truck. Arnold had hired a local man who had a bigger, newer machine. The man brought along his wife and kids; to drive truck, he said; mostly it was to get in on the excitement. Even Arnold, without ever saying much, worked with a new energy and purpose. We lowered the old wagon boxes down from the machine shed, hooked them up and drove them out to the fields.

I sat on the tractor and waited. It was hot; the kids played and fought in the shadow of the truck. The combine circled the field, chaff streaming in the air. The goggled operator sat up top, looking like a man from outer space. When he gave the hand signal I pulled the wagon up alongside, then hopped in the box and guided the grain as it rushed out of the chute.

I drove the wagon in to the granary. Across the road, a hundred yards away, was the new high school swimming pool and, as I passed, the bronzed life guard turned and stared through dark glasses. The wooden-wheeled, faded wagon jerking along behind me, I pulled down my engineer's hat and stared back.

When I got to the granary Arnold set up the auger and the box. Together we shoveled the wheat out of the wagon down into the box, where the auger, a fifteen-foot metal tube, spun it up into the bins as quickly as we could shovel it. We worked fast, feet sinking in the warm grain.

I made that trip over and over all day long, out to the fields and back. I didn't tire of it: in the broad, golden fields our separate losses had converged and been muted. It wasn't over with Ann; there was part of me that was poised and waiting. But then there was no need to do anything else than wait for the combine to complete its slow circling of the field, to feel the rush of grain beating through my hands, feel the first stirrings of the afternoon wind against my face, to work silently with my uncle, the only sound the rattle of the auger when we lagged behind and the hushing of wheat flowing into filling barns during the long, bright day.

July 18

Dear Gene,

I got your letter two days ago and it's been on my mind
ever since. I have attempted and torn up two replies. I
don't know what to say. I know what a special place Arnold
had come to hold in your life—how hard his death must
have hit you. If I knew of a way to comfort you I would.

I appreciate the emotional costs it takes to write a letter
like that. And I wish you were right about the uses that
loss can be put to. But I'm afraid that all that shaping you
talk of, making art or emblems of it, is a little like those cave
drawings at Lascaux—you can make pictures of the thing

that terrifies you the most, try to control it, demystify it, but finally you've got to go out and face the animal again.

You wrote about his dying alone, unhappy, and how that haunts you. I wish I was wise enough to have a consolation for that. I'm not. All I can do is share your sorrow, your hauntedness, in some way of my own and hope that that pain will find its place, its peace, somehow, as other things have.

Maybe it's good that you're going to Fargo for the auction—I'm sure some of it will be nasty and harrowing, but at least it's something concrete to do about it—sometimes physical details help to close things out. It's a shame that you have to get rid of that beautiful farm. Will you be able to save many things from it?

I would like to see you too, though this is perhaps not the time. Ken and I are moving to a house, can you believe it? It's forty-five minutes from L.A., but it's lovely and we'll have so much more room. Ken can have a studio of his own to work in for the first time. He is getting more jobs and is feeling much happier about things.

I did find the magazine. Yes, I do remember the story. Not the same as the original, but reminded me enough to recall your writing it and that whole time. Which is kind of amazing for I realize how much I blocked out of '67 & '68 —can remember '62 & '63 much more vividly.

When will you be moving? I think it is a great stroke of luck, your finding the teaching job. You've probably been in New York long enough—making a break could be exactly the right thing.

Your letter meant so much to me, Gene—awakened so many things—It's been a year since I've heard from you— not since you called me from Banff. You know that I've always prized your letters, even felt closest to you through them. Hearing from you made it seem as if we'd never *stopped writing and talking. I will be thinking of you out in Fargo and I hope it goes well . . . . I know that it will be a kind of trial, but you've got so much going for you now.*

Love,
Ann

Though it was sent airmail, I didn't get the letter until I had returned from Fargo. It was too late by then; it was like a voice overheard across a room; warm, kind words, but addressed to someone else. I left the letter unanswered.

I spent the entire afternoon working in the apartment. Boxes were pyramided in the middle of the bare, newly waxed floor and at first I attacked them randomly, unpacking coffee pots, lamps, winter coats and canisters of used tennis balls. It was the last week of August and, without curtains, the place roasted in the sun. The phone wasn't in yet either, so there was absolute silence, and I worked without interruption.

At the bottom of a box of books I found an old three-ring blue notebook of Ann's. It was a workbook and she had it neatly divided according to the settlement houses she had worked for. It was a model of organization. I thumbed quickly through it, but found nothing but appointments, schedules, notes from meetings, drafts of proposals, nothing to betray the other sides of that past, except perhaps the familiarity of the even, careful strokes of her hand. I tossed it on a pile of things to be thrown out.

I moved haphazardly from one task to another, taking pleasure in the sweaty work. I had no thought of where I was, until, stopping for a moment while hammering up bookshelves, I looked up at the window expecting to see the jumbled, dark outlines of New York, and saw instead ordered lines of trees, the Gothic buildings of the campus and an expanse of lawn on which the summer light had just begun to ebb.

I was at the door of my place with a bag of groceries when I heard the telephone ringing. I fumbled with keys, got the door open, spilling cans across the walk, and sprinted to the phone. It was Ann.

I stood, phone in hand, lost for any reply. I hadn't heard from her since her letter and now she was calling in the middle of the afternoon.

"Where are you?" I said.

"In New York. My parents are here for a few days and it was my only chance to see them before they leave for Europe."

"You flew all the way from L.A.?"

"Yes."

"Is Ken with you?"

"No, he's not," she said. "I'd like to come out and see you."

"I'd like to see you too," I said, though it was not quite what I meant to say.

"I was a little hesitant about calling . . . when I didn't hear from you after my letter."

"It was a good letter," I said. "It's just . . . when I got back from Fargo I didn't feel like writing anyone for a while."

"Gene . . . ."

"When can you come out?" I said.

"If you're not busy I could come out for the weekend."

"I'm not busy."

"Has your school started yet?"

"No. Next week. Let me check the train times," I said.

I got the schedule and we agreed that she would take a train down on Friday morning.

"And if you could find me a place to stay . . . ." she said.

"Don't be silly. I've got a pull-out couch in my living room."

"That would be all right?" she said.

"That would be fine."

When I hung up the phone I gathered up my scattered groceries, put them away, and went out for a walk. I had been almost curt with her on the phone and thinking about it made me angry. Why had I needed to bluff? Everything had changed since I had written her that desperate letter right after Arnold's death; then I had wanted to see her, establish contact with someone, perhaps anyone; since I had returned I had had scarcely a conscious thought about her. It had been three years since I'd last seen her in Berkeley. Everything we had been to one another had been able to exist in a separate world, unthreatened. Yet there was no way I was going to say no to seeing her. There were too many lines of force that demanded it; still, the thought of meeting her again, on strange ground, grated on me like a file on a padlocked door.

The Friday noon train was packed with students returning for the fall semester and they bristled with suitcases, backpacks and tennis rackets. Ann was one of the last people off the train. She didn't see me at first and there was a precious second for me to watch her unobserved. There seemed to be a softness about her that pleased me; I could imagine how I had been attracted to her.

When she saw me she laughed. She moved quickly, almost skipped towards me. At first I made no gesture and she stopped short, misinterpreting.

"Find you a redcap?" I said. She smiled again and I

leaned over and kissed her. She ran the tips of her fingers over my cheek.

"You shaved your beard," she said.

"I told you that," I said.

"No," she said. "It's a nice face."

We had to walk through the campus to get to my apartment and as we walked she told me about their new house and details about her life in California. There were things I had been thinking all morning of saying, but they seemed out of place now; instead I pointed out the sights and asked questions.

When we came through a Gothic arch into a small courtyard I pointed up to a pair of leaded windowpanes. "That's where I work," I said.

"That's your office?" she said.

"Picturesque?"

"It's wonderful," she said. "Let me see it."

"It looks a lot better from down here," I said. "It's very plain, really."

"Still I'd like to see it."

"Okay."

We walked up the narrow three flights of stairs. I opened the door and Ann entered first. It was a small office and cluttered, though I'd been in it less than a month. There were piles of books, papers and manuscripts, a few theater posters leaning against the wall, and letters and correspondence heaped on the desk. The room was warm with sunlight and a half-dozen wasps drifted outside the window, basking in the reflected heat.

Ann went to the window and looked down on the courtyard with its birch trees and bird-spattered gargoyles, the students passing beneath us. "It's nice here," she said. "I'd forgotten how nice it can be on a campus."

"I know," I said.

She turned suddenly. "So I haven't ruined your life, after all?" She said it as if she was trying to make a joke.

"No, you haven't," I said.

She moved away from the window and looked at the picture on the wall. "When did you get this?" she said.

"When I was in North Dakota for the auction," I said. "It was in a pile of stuff they were planning to sell. I lifted it."

Ann took it from its place on the wall to look at it. It was an old photo, cracked and yellowing. It was of my grandmother and two other country women, infants in their arms and children clustered around them. Arnold was there, an eight-year-old boy in knickers, and my mother stood beside him, regarding the camera suspiciously with six-year-old eyes. Newly planted trees partially framed them, but behind were fences and beyond that, blurred and indistinct, the flat, endless horizon. What had drawn me to the picture was its insistent formality, the people clustered proudly together in the open, unprotected space, as if they were held together by the rough, worn, almost mannish arm of my grandmother holding her child.

"I'm sorry that I never got to see it," Ann said. "I thought about you out there this summer."

"It wasn't very long. Five days."

"Is everything done?"

"The land isn't sold yet, but that's being all set up. All the stuff was sold at the auction."

"Did it go well?"

"Go well? Oh, ya, it was a big success. Big picnic . . . three hundred people crawling all over the place, lasted all day . . . and they sold everything. Piles of old newspapers, radios, sold a chopping block for ninety bucks . . . . Turns out that a lot of that stuff is antique. How do you like that?"

"What happened?"

"What do you mean?"

"To Arnold."

I looked at her angrily. "I don't know."

"But you must."

"There's nothing to know. Someone had heard the dog barking in the barn several days in a row and called the sheriff. They came and broke into the house and found him."

"You knew it would happen, didn't you?"

"No, I didn't."

"You must have had thoughts about it."

"I have no thoughts about it." That was a lie. The truth was more like the opposite; that I had many thoughts; that again and again I had thought of him dying alone, at the end of winter; thought back to the end of the harvest when he had invited me to stay and I had said I couldn't, that I had other things waiting; that I had thought and struggled to wrest sense and will out of that loss. But I wasn't going to tell her that; that grief was private; not available for confession.

"He was a very kind man," I said. "Very kind to me. Let me put that back." I put the picture back on the wall. "What about Ken?" I said.

"What about him?"

"Did he know that you were coming to see me?"

"Yes," she said. "He's very easy about things like that. He's not the kind of person who makes a lot of demands."

"He must make some."

"Some," she said. She looked at me, startled, as if I had been told something I couldn't possibly know. "He wants to have a child." I stared at her dumbly. "I know," she said. "It scares me. I don't know if I can go through with it. I don't know why. It's just that having a child seems so final."

"And what about your freedom?"

"That never was what it could have been. It's not like it was."

"No?" I said. She looked at me angrily without answering. "Do you love him?" I asked, more softly.

"Yes, I love him," she said. "He's a very good man. But so were you. And I think about what happened to that...."

"Are you thinking about leaving him?" I asked. I stared at her; she didn't answer. I moved around her, then, almost shouting: "Are you?"

"Gene, I don't know."

"You can't even be thinking of coming back to me. You understand? Don't even think it!"

"I'm not trying to ...."

"Listen to me! When I was in Fargo and saw all those people dismantling my past ... it was very specific, like they were walking off with it, piece by piece ... and I thought for a moment that I could keep it. Keep the farm. The hell with 'em. But I was wrong. I couldn't. It was impossible. You can't do that. You can't hold onto what's gone."

"Gene, I know."

"Have a child, or don't. That's between you and him. Not me." She couldn't stand it any longer; she moved suddenly away from the window and I moved with her. I grabbed her shoulder and without knowing who made the first gesture, we embraced. I held her head in my hands, pressed her against my chest, and then, just as quickly, held her away from me.

"I'm sorry," I said. "I didn't mean ...."

"It's just that I'm afraid ...." she said.

She knelt in a chair, crying, her hands over her face, trying at first to strangle the sobbing, making small, choking sounds, and then not trying to stop it. I turned away from her. The room was brilliant with autumn light; I could hear the wasps bumping against the glass. I turned back to say something, but couldn't speak. I touched her hair softly, gathering it and letting it go, touching it again. The pain of watching her became unbearable, as if the light itself were turning to hard shafts of shining stone, folding in on me. I moved behind her and put my hands on her back. I could feel her sobbing with my hands, its rising and falling. I didn't look at her; there were birds fluttering on the bell tower. I pressed my hands tighter on her back and I felt a shudder go through her, as if something had passed through us both. We sat without speaking for a long time.

"I can't go on doing this, can I?" she said.

"No," I said.

"I couldn't give you up before," she said. "I knew how selfish it was. I just couldn't do it."

"Neither could I," I said. "Let's go outside. We'll take a walk."

After we had taken a long walk along the canal we came back into town and went into a small coffee shop. We sat in a booth, both of us silent and tired. Across from us was a table of students where a rosy-cheeked kid in a blue blazer was telling animated stories; everyone was laughing easily.

"They seem so young," Ann said.

"They are," I said. "They've got it very together, you know?"

"What do you mean?"

"They've got it figured out."

"Mmm. Now they do."

"There's a party tonight," I said. "A friend of mine is

leaving for Japan. We could go, if you're up for it . . . ."
"I think I'll go back," she said. "Is there another train this afternoon?"
"Ya. There's one tonight too, if you wanted to have dinner."
"I think I'll go back this afternoon," she said.
"Okay," I said.

The shuttle train was waiting for us by the time we got to the station. I carried her suitcase into the car and set it up in the rack. I fingered the dirty, frayed upholstery. Ann looked up at me. A dour-looking conductor pulled the whistle.

I leaned over to kiss her and she reached up and took my face in her hands. "I'm glad that I came," she said. "So I can have an idea how you live. It helps to have a picture in your head." She tapped her forehead with a finger, smiling. I leaned forward again, but she turned away.

The conductor pulled the whistle a second time. I stood up, looked at him, then looked back at Ann. Her face was pressed to the window. I pushed quickly by the conductor and onto the platform, walking away without looking back, not even when I heard the train pulling away.

I walked up through the campus alone, through court-yards where eighteen-year-olds tossed Frisbees and hard rock throbbed from a dozen windows. It was late enough in the afternoon that the shadows from the Gothic spires stretched farther and farther eastward across green lawns. I began running up the long steps toward the arch. At the top I stopped, out of breath. The sun threw a double shadow of me, one beside me, on the steps, and the other on the wall behind me. I felt a curious elation.

ABOUT THE AUTHOR

Jim Magnuson was born in Madison, Wisconsin, in 1941, and spent his childhood in small towns in the Midwest. He attended the University of Wisconsin both as an undergraduate and as a graduate student in English. After getting his M.A., he came to New York, where several of his plays were produced in Off-Off-Broadway theaters. For the past four years he has been Hodder Fellow and Resident Playwright at Princeton University.